JIM CRACE

# CONTINENT

published by **Pan Books**
*in association with* Heinemann Ltd

First published 1986 by William Heinemann Ltd
This Picador edition published 1987 by Pan Books Ltd,
Cavaye Place, London SW10 9PG
in association with Heinemann Ltd
9 8 7 6 5 4 3 2
© Jim Crace 1986
ISBN 0 330 29964 6
Printed and bound in Great Britain by
Richard Clay Ltd, Bungay, Suffolk

Individual parts of Continent were first published in the
New Review, London Magazine, Quarto, London Review of Books
and Encounter.

The author is grateful to West Midlands Arts
for financial assistance.

*'There and beyond is a seventh continent – seven peoples, seven masters, seven seas. And its business is trade and superstition.'*

Pycletius, Histories, IV, 3

# One

# Talking Skull

Consider your inheritances, fellow students. Enumer-ate and evaluate. You are the sons and daughters of rich men. Who else but rich fathers could spare the money for tuition fees, for examination bribes, for graduation robes? Calculate the value of those family businesses – the import/export companies, the truck and bus firms, the riverside farming enterprises, the chicken and egg fran-chises, the Rest House chains, the strings of market booths. Include, also, the lands in town and country, the houses in the New Extension, the investments in foreign banks. Subtract all personal bequests and divide the remainder by the number of sons and daughters born to your parents. And there you have it, a nice fat sum, your inheritance. Do not wish your parents dead. Long life and wisdom to them all. But be carefree – they cannot live for ever and, when they die, your comforts are assured. You are the legatees of thoroughly modern businessmen. You inherit wealthy manners, expensive accents, extravagant partialities. You talk of trips to Paris and New York; you sat in cafés, unembarrassed, and ordered wines and beers and shallow cups of coffee in French and English; you talked politics and business and literature; you made liaisons; at private dinner parties you were at ease with artichokes and avocadoes, with cigars and charades. For you this is one world. You are internationalists. This, too, is your inheritance. There are no frontiers to your ambition.

\*

I love so much to meet your fathers. They are unhurried. They are gently inquisitive. 'Do I detect a forest accent, Lowdo?' they ask me. 'What are your family? Timber or farming? Who is your father? How many men does he employ? How many acres?' We sit and contrive between us answers which invent a wide flat valley, a leisurely shoulder-deep river, a contented village of a thousand compounds. Six thousand acres of fertile ground provide nourishment for plantations of black-bark tarbony, fields of maize and sunflower, herds of milk cattle. At the benevolent centre of this paradise, my conjured father, his accountant and estate manager discuss agricultural strategies. From the airstrip a modest Cessna takes off for supplies. A pretty maid serves iced mint-water and honey cake. In the paddock my mother and sister canter on thoroughbreds.

'Where does your father purchase his supplies?' your fathers ask me. 'Who markets his milk? Who buys his corn oil? Who processes his tarbony? Does he own his own mills or is the timber floated down-river and auctioned to merchants? Who handles his affairs in the city?' These are questions I cannot answer. I shrug at your fathers and protest my ignorance. I do not have a head for names and figures, I tell them. I am too immersed in my studies, in the intricacies of Biology. 'Why then,' they insist, 'is your father unknown to us? Does your father never come to the city? Our house is his house. Bring him to us. Let him see that his son keeps good company. Promise us, Lowdo, that you will bring your father to us.'

I cannot satisfy their suspicions. But I cross my legs and let them note expensive Rome-cut trousers, Spanish leather shoes. I rest my hands on the arms of their cane sofas and display the discreet and sparkling bracelet and the gold watch. Certainly my father is rich. Certainly I am from the country – consider my weather-beaten forehead, my tough hands, my plosive accent. There is no concealing wealth and there is no concealing ancestry. If your fathers mistrust my sketch of life at home, then they do not care to press me or to embarrass me. 'Lowdo is a dreamer,' they say. 'Either that or he has something to hide. Something governmental. Something military. Something worth a lot of money, that's for sure. There's gold on his land, maybe. Or orichalc. What a catch for some girl! All the time his inheritance multiplies. Our door is always open to young Lowdo.'

\*

Young Lowdo travels home once a year, fellow students, during the Harvest Vacation, while you are holidaying at your cottages on the Mu Coast or flirting in Manhattan. There is the wide, flat valley which I have described and the lazy river. But still I am a long day's journey from my homelands. I spend the night in the Rest House. The lorries go no further than here. The pretty maid that I have described to your fathers is not a complete concoction. She serves at the Rest House and sleeps with the lorry driver. I cannot say who lives in the large house with the veranda. There are no thoroughbreds, there is no airstrip. But this *is* paradise. When I was a child, I always thought so – the yellow cobs of maize, the golden discs of sunflower, the fat and perfect cows.

At dawn I leave my sleek city clothes with the warden and, dressed in a country tunic and sun cap, set off up the valley on a hire-mule. After a dozen kilometres (tired already, irritable) I leave behind the gummy smells of the tarbony plantations and climb through odourless thickets of thorn and acacia. Lizards scurry and freeze like sniff dancers on a wedding day. The cattle here are slimmer and more restless: their tails slap flies, their leather mouths and stomachs grind thorn needles and dry grass. They will not budge for the mule. They give way to nothing except the secret whistle of the cattle boy. These are the Belted Aurochs of the scrub-people, a chocolate-brown breed of cattle with a broad black waist. Their milk is rich in butterfat but their beef is slow to mature. Their dung spits and glows in the fire. Their hides are tough and oily – good only for buckets or shoes. Their cheese is as greasy and pliable as beeswax and tastes of wood.

The rich landowners of the valley keep away. They have no interest in these modest cattle and this worn land. Belted Aurochs are a poor investment. The riverine cattle are fatter, more docile, more fertile. But here the herd is still the great provider – food and fuel, rough clothing and manure. No family can hope to survive without a dozen or so grazing cows with annual access to a bull. None tries. All are happily obsessed by livestock. Every beast is woven an intricate necklace of straw with its family signature of knots and loops. Tucked into each necklace, like a sporting favour, is a sprig of mullein to protect the cattle from sickness and sorcery. Mullein poultices are strapped to sore udders. Petals from the tall yellow spikes of mullein flowers are added reverently to cheese. Nowhere are there more superstitious people or more pampered animals. Nowhere in the land are there farmers less wealthy.

Your fathers shake their heads and marvel at my watch and bracelet and expensive clothes and extravagant education. If they could see me now, fellow students, on a mule amongst my neighbours, answering their greetings, skirting their lethargic cattle, then they would wonder even more at the source of my riches. Would they welcome me into their homes in this stiff tunic and peasant hat? Would they welcome my father if he came to town?

*

At the last village before the descent into the hollow where our family land is sited, I am called by the small son of a villager and led into their compound for refreshment. My hire-mule is watered and tethered well away from a tempting patch of tomatoes, melon and mullein. I am brought a bowl of perfumed water and a small pat of guest-soap. The boy serves sweet mint tea and dishes of yoghurt and cucumber. They want to know about life in the city. I describe domestic refrigerators and air-conditioned stores, traffic and cinemas, tinned food and night clubs, golf courses and elevators. I offer American filter cigarettes. All – from the boy to the grandmother – accept and puff on them studiously.

'Did you go to the night club?' they ask.

'Yes, many times. I was the guest of my friends' fathers. We had reserved tables close to the stage. There was a beautiful singer from Rome. There was an orchestra. There was an exotic dancer who took most of her clothes off and did cartwheels amongst the customers. There was dancing and girls to dance with.'

'Did you dance, Lowdo?'

'No, not with the girls. But once I got drunk on French wine and danced a country egg dance for them, right there on the stage, with the spotlight on me and the orchestra struggling for a tune. I broke a dozen eggs and a wine glass, but nobody cared. You can behave how you want in a night club. That's what they're for. Everything is allowed so long as you can pay. The eggs and wine glass were on the bill.'

My hosts are happy at the thought of my broken eggs in the city. I am hugged and kissed, my hair ruffled, my cheek pulled. Here it is not a *faux pas* to touch.

'We have a fully suckled calf for your father,' I am told by the mother, her thin arm resting intimately across my shoulder. 'Will you take it with you now? The herd are restless. We have her tied in the shed but still the herd are restless. They know she's there.' She takes a large round cheese and places it, in a cloth, on the ground at my feet. 'This is for your father,' she says, 'if he will take this calf.'

'Let me see the animal,' I say.

She leads me out of the compound to a shed well away from the house and pulls back the leather from the door. The young heifer is brought into the open. I kneel to examine her. Her genitals are badly malformed, her vagina wide and exposed with an enlarged clitoris and a stringy tuft of vulval hair. Her udders are undeveloped. A fold of skin – a rudimentary penis – runs from her udders to her naval. She is a freemartin, the malformed, cursed, and sexually disruptive twin of a bull calf. She is the warped demon of fertility. I tie her lead to the saddle of the mule (she tries to mount him, to excite him) and set off for my father's compound and his herd of ninety freemartins.

*

'Chatter, chatter,' says my father. 'Is that all you've picked up in the city?' He unwraps the neighbour's cheese and holds it to his nose. 'Hmm, too fresh.' He has been spoiled, not liberated, by wealth. He is unlike your fathers. Mean and cunning in outlook, tough, violent in his own defence, narrow-minded, readily pleased and easily offended, unloving. He bullies me with his ignorance. I bully him with my learning. I hold out a textbook. (He doesn't read, of course.)

'So this is chatter? The education that you've bought me, all the latest wisdoms – just "Chatter" to you! Listen!' I read from the book: ' "Twins in cattle have common membranes and a common blood supply. In nine out of ten of all cases where a heifer is twinned with a bull calf, the male hormone of the bull is thought to prevent normal development of the reproductive organs of the female or freemartin calf. Their gonads tend to resemble non-functionary testes, their fallopian tubes and uterus are frequently only partially developed . . ." '

'Chatter,' says my father. Outside, in the long-shadowed dusk, ninety-one freemartins, recreant and degenerate, nuzzle stooks of scrub grass.

'There's nothing strange or magical or ill-omened about these cows,' I tell him. 'Listen to the book! There is . . . a . . . simple . . . biological . . . explanation! They're just unlucky twins.' My father rubs his palm with a forefinger to signal Money. He sweeps his hand grandly round the room to indicate his riches: the cluster of highly polished paraffin lamps, the ornate and ever-silent Italian accordion

10

with its silver trim and mother-of-pearl decoration, the radio (batteries long dead), the bottles of brandy and Negrita, the rugs and tapestries, the clocks and mirrors, the grandiose safe which was brought by my grandfather from the city in a donkey cart in 1934. He flashes gold teeth, gold rings and a gold key to the family safe.

'Chatter,' he says.

In the morning a young man wrapped in a blanket is found sleeping on our veranda. My father wakes him and feeds him with sour bread and cheese and weak mint tea. The young man is soon to be married and has come to buy freemartin milk. My father, like a merchant selling bicycles or typewriters, lists the properties of his product. For centuries his family has been supplying young men with freemartin milk, he asserts. He provides only the best, unwatered and fresh. He gives good measure for a fair price. He has a family reputation to maintain. Potency is a complicated matter. He is a simple man and cannot explain its intricacies. But this has been proven by thousands of satisfied customers: freemartin milk makes all the difference to a nervous young man on his marriage night. It does the trick. None return dissatisfied or with complaints that the milk is powerless.

'Sip this on the morning of your marriage,' he says, producing a grimy jar, 'and your wife will have no regrets. And when you want to have children, come back and buy some more. You will have sons.' The young man hands over a tight bundle of bank notes. He and my father embrace. My father pours him a mouthful of rough spirit for the journey and presents him with the jar of freemartin milk.

11

Two women have been watching from a clump of aloes and, once the bridegroom has gone, they call my father, covering their faces with their shawls. They are sisters. They are barren. Both have been married for eight years. They have loving husbands. 'But we have no children.' My father advises them. 'Infertility is a complicated matter,' he explains. 'I am an uneducated man. I cannot understand its intricacies. All I can understand is the evidence of my own eyes and what I have learnt from my father, my grandfather, my great-grandfather – all noble men. Drink my milk during your periods. Make your husbands sip a little, too, before you sleep together. You will have children.' I look at the women's thin ankles, their slight and bony figures, their heavy-knuckled hands and stiff fingers tugging at their shawls. 'And eat plenty of fruit,' I want to tell them. 'Fresh meat. Green vegetables. Cheese. Plain, cheap cow's milk. You need protein, vitamins, and iron. Then you'll have children.'

One of the women hurries forward to the open ground between the aloes and our house. She puts money under a stone and returns to her less bold sister. My father touches his chest at the spot where his unscientific prejudices imagine his heart to be located and gives thanks. He walks forward to exchange the money for jars of grey milk. Now the sisters scurry forward together, collect their purchases and depart.

In the evening a man of my father's age arrives on an almost white mule. My father lights all his lamps to mark the importance of his guest, an old friend and the head of a respected family. Together they drink deep glasses of spirit and gently mock my studies at the university, my stiff city manners, my closely shaven face.

'You have become a talking skull,' the friend tells me. My father chuckles. 'What? You don't know the story?' Of course I do. It is a folk-tale so familiar to every schoolchild in every continent that even hard-pressed teachers no longer tell it. But the man inhabits a less complicated universe than the schoolroom. He is committed to his tale. Nothing can stop him now. He settles back into the cushions and drains his glass. 'There was a young man,' he says, 'just like you. He left his father and his herd and his neighbours in his home village and went off to the city. Life would be easier there, he thought. Nobody heard from him for over a year. His face was forgotten. No word came to his father, or even to the girl who was his sweetheart. And then, one day, he showed up. Dressed like an American. Full of himself and his new lifestyle. And what a tale he had to tell! You'd think he'd discovered paradise. He boasted that he had found enlightenment in the city. "Nonsense!" they said. "There are no new wisdoms. All wisdoms are old." But this young fellow thought he knew best. "Not so," he said. "Listen to what has happened to me. I was walking in the city one night. I was lost. I was a little drunk. I found an old skull hidden in some bushes. I lifted it up and asked, 'What brought *you* here?' And the skull replied! It said, 'Talking brought me here.' Have you ever heard of such a marvel? I came straight back to the village to tell you about the skull that talks."

'Well, his father and friends had a good laugh. "The city

has gone to your head," they told him. "Did you get knocked down by a lorry? Or is the city drink too strong for you?" But the young man was insistent. What did they know about the big, wide world? He'd show them up for what they were! Ignorant bumpkins. He'd bring the skull to the village. Then they would eat their words. "Bring it, then," an uncle told him. "But don't forget the way you have insulted us. Don't come back without your talking skull or you will bring shame on yourself and your family."

'So he returned to the city. He went to the spot where he had found the skull and, yes, it was still there, exactly as he had left it. "What brought you here?" he asked. Silence. Silence. "What brought you here? What brought you here?" Still the skull was silent.

'Our clever young friend returned each day and tried to strike up conversation. No luck. What could he do? How could he return home without his talking skull? How could he remain in the city without the support of his family? All he could do was persist with the skull. He went without food and work and shelter. Nobody helped him. Why should they? He was a stranger, a crazy stranger who talked to bones. "What brought you here? What brought you here?" He got hungrier. Dirtier. Thinner. Weaker. More desperate. And then, of course, he died, dropping to the ground next to the old human skull. Now, at last, it opened its yellow jaws and asked, "What brought you here?" What do you suppose the young man's corpse replied?'

'Chatter,' says my father.

14

' "Talking brought me here",' I recite dutifully.

My father's friend has embarrassed me to hide his own embarrassment. His is more than just a social visit. He has come on business. His passions are in tumult. On the one hand, he is a man shamed by a wife so sick of pregnancy that she refuses to share his bed. On the other, he is a vaunting lover with designs on a local widow. How to succeed with this woman, half his age? 'Let me take something with me, old friend,' he says, 'to win her heart.' My father makes a great show of thought and then he advises a cunning double application of freemartin milk. What else?

'Passion between men and women is a complicated matter,' he explains. 'Who can unravel such a tangle? My milk can help – but who can say why or how? You'll make your head ache looking for answers. Just trust in the experience of a thousand others. Take one jar for your widow. Add it secretly to her fresh milk. She will begin to think of love. But her love will be indiscriminate. My milk cannot work miracles. I cannot make her prefer you to all others. But if you are constantly there, well then, when she grows tender you will have the advantage. The second jar is for your wife. Maybe she will reconsider.'

My father's friend takes bank notes from his saddle bag and puts them under the almost empty bottle. 'Make sure you give me only the freshest and richest milk,' he says.

It is almost midnight and these two old friends drag an unwilling freemartin out of her sleep and into the light of the stables. She is ugly and malformed and resentful. My father stoops and tugs at her shrunken udders. He works

15

hard in his own shadow, his back blocking his friend's view. Eventually he turns to show a bowl half full of some opaque liquid, a little urine, perhaps, mixed with thick bovine secretions. The cow's udders are rough and sore. My father applies a poultice of mullein and then stands to display what he has managed to coax from the cow's vestigial teats. 'Milk,' he says. 'Good and fresh!'

'Freemartins don't produce milk,' I say. 'They can't and they don't.'

Both men chuckle. 'Talking skull,' says my father.

*

Today a helicopter has been circling the village. It lifts a dust devil of dry earth and grass in its path. Foxes, owls and night voles which should be sleeping in holes and hollows flee from the helicopter's storm of agitated air. The pilot is searching for a level landing spot. The machine settles at last on the edge of the village. Its engine is cut and all that can be heard for a moment is the complaint of a calf separated from the herd. All the villagers have hurried to touch the machine. It is the first aircraft to have landed here.

A woman climbs from the helicopter. She has an old tanned face and young blonde hair. Who speaks German or English or French, she wants to know.

'English,' I say. 'Some French. I am at your service, of course. *Je ne demande pas mieux. Cela va sans dire.*'

'Excellent. Tell me, do you know the man who has the herd of freemartin cows?'

'He is my father.'

Now she is delighted. She holds out a broad hand. 'My name is Anna,' she says. 'And yours?'

'Lowdo.' ('Lowdo, Lowdo,' repeat my neighbours, recognising a word.) She is a Swedish film-maker, she says. She is making a documentary. Would it be possible to film in the village, to talk to my father, to see the freemartin herd? I turn and ask my neighbours. Yes, yes, they say. Let her film in the village. Our house is her house. Now she introduces the pilot, her cameraman and her sound recordist. They grin and wave as I translate their names and their occupations.

'Who'd like a ride in the helicopter?' the pilot asks. 'You could see your village from above.' Nobody volunteers.

I lead Anna and her crew along the track to our compound. She is animated and delighted with every-thing she sees. She makes notes. She asks the names of flowers and small children. I explain the significance of the cattle necklaces and help her with the pronunciation of some common words. She is, she says, interested in living folklore. She has filmed in thirty countries but still she hasn't lost her sense of wonder. 'As soon as I heard just half a whisper of this freemartin business,' she says, 'I just dropped everything and flew right out. It's all so magical, so naïve.' But, no, she isn't criticising. Naïvety she admires. It is a quality missing in Sweden. Have I ever visited Stockholm? No? Then it must be arranged. She will talk about it to a man she knows at the embassy. But first she asks for all my help with her film. Will I do that for her? Will I persuade my father to agree to the filming?

17

My father is unimpressed (or so he claims) by the fuss and commotion. It is all inconvenient. Already, he complains, customers have been scared away. He has lost money; he has lost time; his milk does not last for ever; the clatter of the helicopter has upset his herd.

'Tell him that this film is very important to us,' instructs Anna.

'Ask her how important,' says my father.

Anna offers fifty American dollars but they are worthless away from the city and the banks. My father points at the bags and boxes of the film crew. Each one is opened. He inspects cameras and lenses and film cans. Clothes and camping gear are unpacked and displayed. He touches a hurricane lamp, a camping stove, a torch, an inflatable mattress, and the aluminium tent-poles. These are his fee. Anna nods: 'Tell your father that these are our gifts to him when we leave. These are his only when all the film is in the can.'

I work hard for Anna and her film. My father is not easily managed. He does not understand the requirements of the cameraman. He does not have the patience for the repetitions of filming. But he has set his heart on the tent-poles and is grumpily co-operative. He is filmed selling milk to a shy bridegroom. He is filmed feeding the herd. I translate Anna's questions to him and paraphrase his rough answers for the film's sub-titles. I arrange for the film crew to visit a woman who says she was barren before she took my father's milk. Now she is pregnant and has a two-year-old son. I coax the cattle to remain still while the camera examines their organs and udders.

In the evening Anna stands me with my back to the herd and my face to the camera and asks me to talk about my childhood. I recount the loneliness of life without mother, brothers or sisters. I describe long days spent watching the herd. And short, happy days as a schoolboy at the college in paradise valley.

'Talk of the freemartins,' says Anna. 'Are they sacred to the people here? What is the magic of their milk? Tell it in your own words. Tell us what you learned as a child.'

'They're not sacred,' I say. 'They upset the herds, that's all. They're eccentric. They're licentious. They're lunatic cows. People fear them. And where there is fear there is also superstition. It all began generations ago. Nobody can say how and why.'

'Can *you* suggest how and why?'

'People like to be reassured,' I say. 'They like to believe that solutions to problems can be bought by the jar.'

'But when your father dies, you will follow the tradition of your family and take over the herd?'

I squint into the sun and shake my head. I stand, dear friends in the city, at the centre of my inheritance. Now, at last, you see it. Intangible. Incredible. Uncashable. Each year my father hands me bundles of bank notes from the safe and packs me off to the city and the university. He does not grasp the meaning of this money. All he understands is the ritual of transaction. All that he expects in return is that, when he is old, I will come back to his hollow of land and pummel these barren teats for local rewards. His is wealth at the expense of science. His are riches that exile freedom. What must I do, fellow students? Decay here by the light of a thousand oil lamps? Or cast off my inheritance, remain with you and your fathers, put my faith in science and modernity?

'I will not accept the burden,' I say to the camera and the people of Sweden. 'My father is the last in line.'

\*

Your fathers have been solicitous. Still I am invited to their tables at night clubs and to their air-conditioned lounges at home. They serve freshly-ground coffee from Colombia and delicate liqueurs from farflung airport shops. Since the television transmission in Sweden I have become a bar-room celebrity. My photograph has appeared in local papers. One government minister condemns my people for their barbarous superstition. Another applauds them for their sense of tradition. A zoologist on the radio argues that the isolation of freemartins makes good sense as their presence unnerves the docility of cows. Another claims that they should be prized above all others as they are good beef cattle, putting on meat with eunuch ease. A scientific commission should be formed, he says, to investigate ways of breeding freemartins. Rival editorials in the newpapers call either for Government Help to Protect National Traditions or for A Battle Against Quackery. It is no longer possible for me, fellow students, to hide my inheritance from you. I abandon my reticence. Instead, I exaggerate my lofty manner and the precision of my dress. I have my hands manicured, and powder my forehead. I grow a moustache in the European fashion. I suppress my tell-tale *p*s and *b*s. Any inquiries about the herd I refer to my father. It is his business, not mine. My business is the mastery of Biology.

It is *your* father, Feni, who suggests the rationalisation of my inheritance. 'Don't sniff at money, Lowdo,' he tells me, 'especially your own. Remain intimate with your wealth. You want to be a city boy with an office, a bank account, and a Peugeot. You admire scientific curiosity, business initiative, modern industriousness. But all our business fortunes are based as much as yours on superstition. What is superstition but misdirected reverence? Your clients overvalue bogus milk. Ours overvalue transistors, motor cars, fashionable clothes, travel. This is the key to business. Unearth what is overvalued, amass it, and sell at inflated prices. Your forefathers were the first of the modern businessmen. They grasped this basic principle of trade. You should be boastful, not shamefaced. What will you do? Renounce your inheritance and its possibilities and live in modesty here? How will you survive? Where will you work? Who needs biologists in a city of trade?' He points at my polished shoes, my expensive jacket, my jewellery, the weightless antique coffee cups on the glass-top table, at you, Feni, sitting quietly in your best silk dress in the courtyard with a Parisian magazine. 'What will become of this?'

And so he advises me to modernise, to deputise, to expand. 'When your father dies,' he says, 'keep the herd, but stay here in the city, a free man, at ease, comfortable, amongst your own kind, and run those freemartins, as a business.'

'But the milk is no good!'

Your father laughs. 'This coffee is no good,' he says. 'It makes my heart race. It tastes bitter. Why do I drink it? Habit and superstition. I believe it sobers me when I have been drinking. I believe it sharpens me up when I am tired. I believe that an offer of coffee to friends equals the hospitality of a thousand welcomes. You and science would tell me that coffee doesn't sober, doesn't relax, doesn't revive, doesn't welcome, that it shortens my life, costs a fortune, disrupts the economy of Brazil, and if left too long in the coffee pot will corrode the silver. But try to stop me drinking it! I don't care for the dictatorship of science. Nor do your neighbours. Freedom of choice. Deceive yourself at will, that's the motto of the nation. Harness superstition. Turn it to your advantage. Milk it dry!'

*

Nowadays I do not dream of the wide valley and the ragged heads of sunflowers but of a white, cool office with banks of telephones and the clatter of tills and typists. I see myself with friends in an ante-room. I rehearse long conversations with the fellow students of my own sons and daughters at the university. I am unhurried with them and gently inquisitive. They love so much to sit and talk with me about their studies or their trips to Europe.

I imagine, too, my homelands far off in the scrub. There, a salaried farm-manager minds my herd and sells measured jars of freemartin milk at fixed prices (cash only) to newly-weds and the childless. I see a lorry with my name on its side collecting supplies of milk each month and bringing it to my shop in the city. Freemartin milk and fresh mullein are now available to all. My best customers here are the tourists who, if they are too timid or cynical to invest in a sachet of dried milk, are eager to spend dollars and francs and marks on coloured postcards of the herd and 'lucky' scraps of freemartin hide. I have written and had printed an illustrated booklet on our family and its traditions. It sells well. My dream flowers and expands. My sons and daughters consider their inheritances with placid equanimity.

But in more sober moments I do not dream. I mark time. Each year I visit my father during the Harvest Vacation and contemplate our cattle, infertile and refractory, as they butt and low amongst the tough grasses and the stunted thorns. In the village now they call me Talking Skull. My neighbours are always keen to share my father's jokes. They mean no harm. My father, rather than weakening and ageing, seems to grow stronger and more vigorous. Has he grown a little taller, even? He has no grey hairs. His back is square and straight. His teeth and eyesight have not deteriorated. I fancy that he fears his heirs and has determined to live for ever.

*Two*

# The World with One Eye Shut

The soldiers say that I am fortunate. I have the best cell in the block. Its window (if I stand on my bunk with my head pressed close to the outer wall and one eye shut) allows a view of the outside world, the medley, careless, trading town from which they have removed me. My open eye can follow an angle which cuts across the barracks yard and squeezes between the back of the regimental offices and the pinkstone building which faces on to the town. Beyond is my view, a thin, upright oblong topped by the sky with, once in a while, the ornament of a plane or helicopter or hawk. Diluted in the distance are the hill-top houses where the bigwigs and the lordlings live, the hotels of the bankside district, the trees of Deliverance Park, the river where all of this began.

In the foreground is the wire gate of the barracks. I can see the bustle of the women there, the placards, the photographs of missing sons and husbands, the soldiers and the militia squeezing through on foot and motorbikes to visit bars and brothels in the town, the uniforms, the ministerial and military cars, the plainclothes men.

My sister 'Freti is at the wire gate each evening. I can recognise the exaggerated colours of her wardrobe and the way she stands with her arms crossed over her chest and her chin resting on the back of a hand. I have called to her, ' 'Freti, I'm here.' But that was a waste. How can she hear me beyond the glass at that distance with all the din of the women at the gate, their singing, their cries, and the traffic on Government Drive? I tell myself she's there for me, that she has spotted my thin face and thinner hair framed in this window, that she wears my name on a badge on her chest, that she is one of the women who have embraced the barracks with their jostling demands for family news. But 'Freti stands apart, hanging her face at the edge of the crowd. She's got wall eyes. They float. They pop and bubble. And her mouth hangs loose. She grins. I have caught her, sometimes, snoozing in our yard at home, mouth and eyes shut. Then she is beautiful. But awake, slack faced and vacant, she looks and is a simpleton. She's not the sort to join parades or picket lines. She's at the gate because she's set her heart upon a soldier.

*

What kind of man is he, this Corporal Beyat? 'I know you,' he said, the night they brought me in. 'You've got that witless sister.' I knew his face, too, from that splashing circle of young and skittish conscripts who swam at the river on warm evenings, diving from the cycle bridge or bragging with handstands and cartwheels on the grass. I remember 'Freti standing in the shallows, with her shoes clasped to her chest. She watched the conscripts as they played noisily and roughly in the river. And then, this Beyat had kicked a flirting loop of water over her. It was there, knee deep, with dripping shoes, that her devotion to him began. My mother always told me, 'Keep an eye on 'Freti. She'll do herself some harm one day.' And so I left my colleagues from the legal offices (we had been sitting, carping, on the bank) and beckoned to my sister to leave the water.

And, here, a picture of me, the brother, the nervous clerk, should take its place, my polished shoes six inches from the river, my voice just audible, my manner prudent, cautious, sly – the perfect citizen of a town where jeeps and empty market stalls, sweeping motorcades of politicians in black Panache saloons and a garrison of tough and narrow conscripts made the streets wayward with apprehension. And so it was gently that I called again to 'Freti to come ashore. But she would not budge. She did not want the amusement on the faces of the soldiers to be cut short by her departure. She did not want the soldier who had kicked the water to turn his square and guileless face away. She scooped up armfuls of water and soaked her face and clothes to prolong his interest in her. I tried to pull her, but she fell, to general laughter now even from the people on the bank. She was laughing. Even I was laughing; to have shown my anger would have been to make myself visible. They thought I was her boyfriend and splashed me, too, so that we walked home, she and I, dripping wet through the narrowing streets to the district where we lived in tenements as packed and poisonous as hives.

I saw him once again, in uniform and armed, standing at the market bar, talking drill and discipline with his army friends. How would you describe him? Unremarkable, I think. A small potato. A farmer or a trader's seventh son, a country boy ennobled by conscription and his youth. 'Freti was at his shoulder, not quite excluded from their group. She tilted her face and smiled whenever they smiled amongst themselves. That was the way she had spent her life so far, at the edge of groups, cold-shouldered by the troupes of children in our street but tagging along alone unless she was needed as the butt of jokes.

When Beyat made to leave the bar he turned to 'Freti, saluted her and clicked his heels in an extravagant farewell. She held on to his arm without a word and tugged him to her, like a small child weedling for a treat. Beyat prized her fingers loose and shoved her backwards. I half rose from where I was sitting and called to her to come away. I had become expert at such interventions: my tone, my manner, my keenness not to give offence. But she held his arm again, so he picked her up and lifted her to the far end of the bar and sat her down amongst the dirty glasses in a pool of spilt beer. He placed an exaggerated kiss upon her forehead. Was this just play? The soldiers applauded. All the men there were smiling. They thought it was the best of jokes. 'Freti did too. She returned for more. This time he picked her up and sat her on my table. 'She's yours,' he said. 'Take her home . . . and lock her up.' 'Freti held on to Beyat, her hands clasped behind his neck. She loved it when he carried her across the bar. She was quickened by the intimacy of his grip, by the laughing and the passion that he displayed on her account, by that one kiss. I let him lift her once again. He took her from the bar and carried her across the market to the jeep which he had parked in the taxi bay. Would she have thanked me if I had run to save her?

Beyat's friends remained. They had been turned sullen, vulgar, by his departure. They made remarks at his and her expense. Poor old Beyat, they said, he can only make his mark with whores and simpletons. Their minds were on the jeep and on the girl. Heading where and with what in mind? They called out in the bar; rowdy, poor boys from the provinces. (Rich boys, wise boys, lived abroad or were too sickly for conscription.) Stools were toppled. Beer was spilt. That's how young men pass their time when the only girl has gone.

I rose to leave. They blocked the door. Have a drink with us, they said. I shook my head and smiled. Our family always smiles. They brought me a glass of American beer, nevertheless, and put it on my table. 'Thank you,' I said, but I left it there, untouched. If they had not been soldiers, I might have spoken up for 'Freti.

But silence was best. What could protestations change?
'Well, drink it then,' they said, and pointed at the glass. It
tasted far too strong for beer. Cheap spirits had been added
to make what, I believe, is called a Stupor Stew. But I
drank it all, so what?

Once they had left, I excelled myself, I think. I spoke
out. The rush of alcohol had made me careless. There were
some phrases which I had learnt from the legal documents
which I was paid to type. I called the soldiers rogues and
rapists, but in language which only advocates would
recognise. 'Save this town from cullions and caitiffs,' I
said. 'Protect us from the despots who tyrannise our
sisters and make recompense with beer.' There was no
laughter now, except my own. People turned inwards.
They hugged their glasses, raised their voices and pre-
tended that they had no ears. Ours had become a town
which had no ears: the rich built high walls around their
homes and topped their iron gates with wire; bankers and
diplomats drew the blinds on their limousines or travelled,
drably, in disguise. Costers in the market place wouldn't
trade in rumours any more. 'Be deaf, be happy' is what
they said.

*

If I had been calm and in command I would have reminded
Corporal Beyat of that day when he had taken my witless
sister, as he called her, for a ride and she had returned
bruised and ecstatic late at night. But I was crying from the
beating they had given me, and shaking, too, from fear.

'Why am I here?' I asked. He shook his head. 'For nothing much,' he said. 'For talking with your mouth open, like all the others here. That's what happens nowadays if you grumble with your drinks. There's someone paid to listen hard in every bar – and we've lots of room down here for all the big mouths in the town. You'll see.' But he was only talking tough. He knew nothing. Perhaps my name and photograph had appeared one evening on a list and a squad had been sent to seek me out. For what? Perhaps I had been mistaken for another man, one wanted by the police. Perhaps I had simply been unlucky – the wrong face in the wrong place when the word went out there were dissidents at large. A car door had swung open as I was walking from the market with a newspaper and a bag of manac beans. They were expert at abduction. I was pulled on to the back seat and the car was in motion before I had a chance to cry out for help to the old men who sat in the shade of their porches and watched the traffic pass. The beans spilled on to the floor and cushions as expert blows to the chin, hardly hurting, kept me dazed and silent as we drove out of our gaunt and pungent streets to the wide catulpa'd avenues and to my cell.

'Count yourself as lucky,' said Beyat. 'You've got me to keep an eye on you. And this cell, it's got a window, see. You can watch the soldiers marching in the yard. This is a five-star cell. Until yesterday a Government minister was here. They came, they asked some questions, they let him go perhaps. Or he was transferred. No one stays for long.' At his instruction I took off my clothes and watch and packed them in a plastic bag. My five-star cell – a mat, a bunk, a bucket – was no smaller than my room at home. And it was clean and odourless. 'Your sister,' he said, checking between my legs and in my mouth for money, weapons, false teeth, drugs. 'She's no great catch, you know, not for a soldier. We take our pick. If there are girls about, then count me in. But 'Freti, she's got mushrooms for a brain. She got what she was after. And now she should clear off.' He was talking as if we had just met in a bar, conspiratorial strangers, boastful with anonymity and drink. 'Is that why you've brought me here,' I asked, 'to talk about my sister? Does she know I'm here?' He laughed: 'No one knows you're here, that's our job. You've gone missing. You've taken off to join the insurrection. You're dead. You couldn't stand your witless sister any more, so you cut your throat and climbed into a hole.' He handed me some brown overalls and a pair of plastic sandals. 'Put them on,' he said. 'Stop shaking. You're getting on my nerves.'

*

I have stood at the window and watched Corporal Beyat as he goes off duty through the wire gate. The women press forward and shout the names of the sons and husbands who have disappeared. They push leaflets into his pockets. They whisper subversion as he squeezes through them and out on to the open pavement of Government drive. 'Freti tags along without a word from him. Once he turned and shouted, 'Keep away,' perhaps, or 'Leave me alone. You're getting on my nerves.' Might he have mentioned me? He pushed her back. But she took no notice. She had found someone to love and that was that. By the time they had taken ten steps they were out of sight, masked by the wall of the regimental offices, and I could only guess at my sister's insistent courtship, her coquetry, her blandishments, the candour of her face.

I can only guess, too, at what will happen to me here. No one has come to ask me questions. There has been no opportunity for me to clear my name, or to answer any charges or complaints. Those other young men whom I meet in the latrines or in the shower block are firebrands from the university or leafleteers or the sort who pontificate on platforms. They sing defiant songs as they wash. I do not know the words – or tunes. From them I hear about 'the kitchen' where, they say, all prisoners are overwhelmed, stretched out naked on an unhinged door and clipped by ear and toe to magnetos. There are hoods and chains and electric prods. There is a punishment called the crate. Another called the handstand. Sometimes it is silent in the kitchen; that is when, they say, electrodes have been placed upon a detainee's teeth and the current switched on. Then, no one ever screams.

Sometimes I talk to a man who is more my own age. He, too, like me, was taken from the street. But he was carrying posters and a pot of paste. Our only hope, he says, is the women at the wire gate. If only our names could be smuggled those few yards, then we would be safe. Do I know people who could set us free? But others warn me not to answer. They say this man is a soldier in disguise, an informer. Then they engage me, too, in whispers? Which soldiers do I think would take a bribe to carry a note outside or to mutter a name at the gate? To what lawyers in the town should they address their messages? What am I, other than a legal clerk, unmarried, underpaid, unremarkable in every way? What faction do I represent? They do not trust my answers – so I tell them about Beyat, my sister and my hope that he has taken word of me to her. 'You must talk to him,' they say, insisting that I remember all their names. 'Perhaps he will be our postman.'

*

For much of the day I stand on my bunk and look out, with one eye shut, upon the town. I have devised my own clock by the comings and the goings at the gate, by the shifts of soldiers passing through the frontier of wire, by the exercising squads in the barracks yard, by the times when the kerosene lanterns are lit on the nut stalls in the street. I know that when the raffia screen is lifted in the nearest window of the regimental offices, the woman clerk who sits there will light a cigarette to start her working day. A match flares in the glass. I know that when the klaxon calls, conscripts will run across the yard below to queue for their soup and potato at the canteen door. I know which conscripts will squat in a circle, playing dice, which will kick a ball against my wall, and which will sit alone. I know when work is done: the raffia screen comes down again, the office workers and the off-duty soldiers make their way into town, the army chauffeurs button their coats and start the engines of the government cars, and the soldiers at the wire gate push back the women waiting there. There is the woman with the headscarf. She comes at lunch time and stands immobile with an unfurled portrait of a man. There are the white-haired women in the black clothes who have the energy of pedlars, blocking the way of every man who exits, holding up their lists. There is the fat girl with the flag, the tall woman with three children, the bandy one, the girl with short hair, the stocky woman who bangs on the bonnets of passing cars. There is the pulse of flame from their charcoal brazier at night.

*

'How's my sister?' I asked Beyat while he stood and supervised the cleaning of my cell. 'Old Slobberjowl?' he said, and made a gaping, lovelorn face. 'She hangs around outside the barracks. Where I go, she goes. She makes a fool of me.' 'You made a fool of her,' I said. Beyat nodded. He was embarrassed. He was only half to blame, he claimed. She was a temptress for all her innocence. She had clung to him, had she not? She had let him lift her and transport her round the bar. She had behaved, well, like a whore, tugging at his arm and pulling at his uniform. Was he to blame if he had weakened for a little fun? Any soldier in the bar would have done the same, would – so provoked – have carried 'Freti to the jeep and driven off to find a spot amongst the trees of Deliverance Park, where lovers who could not afford a hotel room could lie amongst the shrubs. They did have sex, he said. And endearments were exchanged, polite and intimate as suited such a time, with my sister's bright and grotesque clothes cast off, the soldier tender-tough, intractable, and shanty boys (attracted to the place by the abandoned army jeep) watching and whistling from behind the trees.

'She'd led me on,' he said. 'And I told her so, after we had done. I told her that I had a girl back home. She said it didn't matter, that she could be my girl in town.' Once again he made a gaping, lovelorn face. How could she be his girl in town, with a mouth and eyes like that? He listed all the times when he had turned his back on her, when he had passed her in the street or at the gate. Only once, when he was drunk, and she had trapped him in a bar, defences down, had they visited the Park again, at night. Two other soldiers had come, too. 'See what she has started?' he said, and I believe he could have wept at the anguish that she caused if the captain had not entered at that time and led me to the kitchen.

The reports of the firebrands and the leafleteers had been exaggerated. The room was no more than an office – a desk, a tablelamp, two chairs, a cabinet, a sink. The captain stood behind me at the door. A man in an open-necked shirt sat at the desk with a pile of folders. 'We have some simple questions, then you can be released or transferred to another place,' he said. 'Please sit.' He asked my name, my occupation, my address in the town. And then: 'With which political groupings are you associated?' I told him, None. He nodded and wrote for a few moments. 'Well, we are in no hurry,' he said, 'We will take our time. Come and see me here tomorrow. And in the meantime give some thought to your position. If you will not answer questions then our hands are tied. We might need to be more forceful. Either way, it's up to you, so long as we have answers. Think of yourself – there's no one else to keep an eye on you. No one knows you're here.' 'You're wrong,' I said. 'Perhaps, my sister knows I'm here. She's with the women at the gate.' He smiled. 'My family knows I'm here,' I added. 'The lawyers at my office know I'm here. The women at the gate have all the names.' The captain shook his head. 'You think that it's not possible,' I said. 'We have our postmen. I have friends inside and out who can attest that I am innocent of everything.' I extemporised the petitions and the affidavits that they might expect if I were not released. Once again I used words and phrases which I had typed in legal papers. 'Such bravado,' said the man in the shirt, 'does not impress.' He signalled to the captain that I should leave. The captain led me back along the corridor and up the stairs to my cell. 'Tell me,' he said, 'who are the postmen?' I thought of my splashed clothes, of the beer that I'd been forced to drink, of Beyat and the two soldiers, the parked jeep amongst the trees, 'Freti with her loose eyes and the indelible smile. Was it too late to intervene? 'Who do you think?' I said. 'Who's sleeping with whose sister?'

*

Beyat came again, as I stood on the bunk watching the women at the gate. 'What's going on?' he said. 'What did you tell the captain? He wants to know if there are soldiers who have any contact with the sister of a prisoner. You're going to get a beating if you've played the big mouth once again.' I shook my head. 'Know who's to blame?' he said. 'Your witless sister. You know what'll happen, don't you? I'll get posted to some upcountry dump, thanks to you and her.' I nodded at the window and said, 'You see, she's waiting for you all the time. Sooner or later the captain was bound to know.' He stepped up to stand beside me and look out. 'Press your head against the wall,' I told him, 'and shut one eye.' 'She's there again,' he said. He pushed me up against the wall and jabbed at my stomach with each word: 'And what suggestions has the witless brother got for clearing up this mess?' 'Why don't you let me have a word with her?' I said.

'You have a word with her?' Beyat thought that funny. 'How will you have a word with her? You're in here, and she's out there.' 'I'll write,' I said. He tore a sheet from his report book and handed me a pencil: 'It'd better work!' I wrote five lines and pushed the square of paper into Beyat's uniform pocket. He took it out and read it. I had written, 'Dear 'Freti, I'm in the barracks, in a cell. Corporal Beyat is one of my warders and he will see that I come to no harm. But if he is spotted with you, my sister, then who knows what his officers might think? You place him and me in danger – so, I beg you, if you love us, stay away. Please show this letter to my mother and our friends. Your devoted brother.' 'That might cool her off,' I said, 'though she can't read. You'll have to read it to her.'

Later that day, I watched from the window as for the

first time Beyat acknowledged 'Freti at the gate and they walked off side by side.

★

Within an hour he had returned. The captain brought him to the cell. 'What's this?' he said, holding up the page from Beyat's report book. 'A letter for your postman?' He crumpled up the note and tossed it to Beyat. 'What kind of barracks are we running here?' I looked at Beyat for the answer. Had he gone straight with my note to the captain? Or had they followed him, scooped him from my sister's side, in their expert fashion, as he took the note from his pocket, read my words to her, and pressed it in her hand? And my sister, did she stand, slack-mouthed, wide-eyed and silent as the car with Beyat sped out of sight? Or did she struggle with them in the street, screaming out to leave her love alone? What would she do now that he was gone? Beyat's face said nothing, except that he was fearful and that there were bruises on his cheek and chin. I kept silent, too. I stood with my mouth open and waited. 'Know who you look like? Your witless sister,' he said. He stepped forward and popped the crumpled note into my open mouth. 'That's his mouth,' said the captain. 'What did I say? I said, take it back and ram it down his throat. That was an order. That wasn't pleasantries.' Beyat turned again to me. 'Swallow,' he said. I didn't swallow. I spat it out.

The captain picked up the paper. 'Hold him down,' he said. Beyat pulled my arms behind my back and pushed me to my knees. The captain reached forward and gripped my throat. 'No one knows you're here,' he said. 'No one knows you're here but us.' My mouth was open and my head tipped back. He dropped the paper in. It rested on my teeth and tongue. He took a pencil from his uniform and poked the paper down until it was wedged at the back of my throat, bunching my tongue against my bottom teeth. Again he poked with the pencil, reaching deep with his fingers, sour with nicotine, into my mouth. They brought water from the latrine and tipped it down my throat until my note to 'Freti was beyond reach and the breath from my lungs was blocked and buffeted by the damp paper. 'The prisoner committed suicide,' the captain said. I waved my arms for more water, for more air, but they had gone and closed the cell door behind them. That was to be the last we saw of Beyat. Where did he end up? In a cell, like us, as the shower-block radicals were to claim? Or was he proved right? Was he sent, perhaps, to some dry and joyless outpost, as he had feared, his pay docked, his stripes removed? Was he that lucky?

I will not pretend that I gave any thought to 'Freti or to Beyat as I beat my hands upon the cell door and drowned on paper. My mind was empty. Panic is deaf and blind. I began to cough and did not stop. The paper lifted with every spasm of my throat but fell again as I sucked in air. I tried to push a finger into my pharynx and pull the paper free but the coughing and my tongue prevented me. What could be done, against gravity, against nature, to expel the blockage through my mouth? My breathing took on a pumping rhythm as if I were blowing stomachfuls of air into an aircushion or a child's balloon. First there was spittle on the cell door and then spots of pink and bubbly blood. I turned and stared, red-faced, pop-eyed, into the centre of the cell. There was nothing but the bunk and the window and the rasping in my throat. I was surprised how light the bunk was when I pulled it from the wall and how easily I could lift it to my shoulders and throw it at the door. The effort seemed to ease my breathing. I lifted it again to arm's length above my head and – the one, the first, dramatic gesture of my life – let it fall against the glass of the window.

I must presume that, when the glass fell outwards from my cell and dropped like broken ice into the barracks yard, someone at the wire gate was staring down the channel between the pinkstone building and the back of the regimental offices seeking out the window in my block where, perhaps, a husband or a brother or a son was missing home. When I stood on the upturned bed and looked out on the sky, the trees, the town in the distance, I could see a woman pointing through the gate in my direction. A soldier going out into the town had stopped, too, and was turning. I pushed my head and shoulders out and screamed at all the people. The air, the voice, the paper, the pressure of the window frame upon my chest, the consternation of my lungs, conspired to produce a sound of such velocity and volume that the letter to my sister shot out into the air high above the yard, heavy with saliva, pink with blood, and bounced far beyond the puddles of shattered glass. Now all the placards and the banners of the women were in the air and I could hear them calling to me and see them pressing hard against the wire gate. ' 'Freti,' I screamed. ' 'Freti, 'Freti.' But, in the mêlée of women and the columns of militia running and the first blows struck, I could not detect my sister's vivid clothes.

Then I spotted her, a woman no longer standing back from all the mayhem I had caused (her arms crossed, her chin down, her mouth agape, waiting for a soldier). She was clamouring now amongst the women and calling out a name. Whose name I cannot say. There was too much passion, and too much noise, and I am far too distant from the gate.

# *Three*

# Cross-country

How had they reacted, these people, when the young teacher came to the valley, earnest and eager? Old Loti brought him down to the village on horseback on his second day and took him round to shake grave hands at the mayor's house and informal ones at the village store. People smiled at him smiling and waited until they got to know his particular ways before they showed any warmth to the newcomer, the 'volunteer' from Canada. His pupils due back at school within a week, kept away but watched. The men who had met foreigners before, while working

47

in the mines or in the markets and warehouses of the city, stayed close but silent. Those that shook his hand saw that his horse did not like him and that he sat awkwardly on it and pulled too closely on the reins. The horse was reserving judgment, looking for something to trust, and so would they. Horses knew a lot. Did not the white horse escape the flood which drowned the shepherdess?

They did not see him on a horse again, though all the young men of the mountains rode horses, for on the fourth day, at dusk, Eddy Rivette took his shorts and running shoes from their bag and set off at a soft pace across the compound of the school. He tested the ground and the stones and the thorns until he was sure of them, and then, lengthening his step, turned to the steep ridge which separated his half-valley from that of the village and the store. Alone on the tracks worn by animals and borrowed by men, he encountered everything which he had expected: sunset, warm earth, a sense of liberation amongst a landscape and a people equally dispossessed. He picked his way, running all the time but choosing, heading for landmarks and favouring distance to the hard work of gradients. By the time he was in sight of the store and was surprising those who sat outside, Eddy Rivette had followed for the first time the track which he was to run every day for the fifteen months he stayed in the hills.

'What's that teacher doing, running half-dressed across the hard ground of the hills?'

Old Loti could not give the answer. Men walked or rode in the village but perhaps in Canada they ran in white shorts. He did not know.

'Perhaps in Canada they don't have horses,' he said, and the men nodded that this was so because they remembered how the teacher had sat on his horse two days before.

'Children run,' said the storekeeper. 'They run just for the pleasure of it.'

'Yes, but not alone,' said Loti. 'And anyway, watch him. He doesn't run like a child. He runs as if he has some purpose . . . but without any urgency. That's Canada for you.'

But they got used to it and after a while began to look forward to it, like anything reliable and harmless. Within an hour of the children from the school slowly picking their way down the hillside towards the village at the end of their day, the slim, tense figure of their teacher would appear briefly at the summit of the ridge above the village, disappear into the slip of an erosion gulley and then come in view again lower down the hill where the track was quite flat. There, the teacher came forward on his toes, head down and fists clenched, and ran the last two hundred metres in a sprint, not slowing and stopping until he had passed the smiles and grins of the men who sat at the store. Then he turned, cool and with breath to spare, and smiled himself and said Hello to all who had been watching.

He got to be quite famous. But fame is something different from popularity. It is less demanding for a start and has more to do with talent than virtue. But not even much to do with talent. The fame which Eddy Rivette enjoyed was just that of someone behaving strangely but purposefully in a place where there were enough old men with the leisure to watch. When they smiled and clapped at his daily approach at the store it was not with affection or welcome but at what he was providing for their day. If they had genuinely known and liked him, the running would have embarrassed them. It was strange. It was quirky. It separated them from him. Not to be wished of a friend.

'Isra-kone, however, *was* a friend of the village. He was a young man, uneducated in school ways but knowing and intelligent and, best of all, a fine talker and a great horseman. These two things mattered to the men of the village who were too old to be judged by the recent talents which were taught at the school. 'Isra was one of the last initiates of the valley, having spent twelve days, two of them drugged unconscious, at the circumcision lodge in the mountains. He knew the secret songs in the old Siddilic, drummed endlessly at him and his fellows at the lodge. They had repeated the words, their stomachs pressed to the walls to ease the pains of hunger. After 'Isra's lodge the old mayor had died and the new mayor, old Loti's brother, discontinued circumcision of the young villagers and the lodges and the secret alliances which sprang from them, not because he was modern but because he feared the new directives of the government officers in the city more than he feared the criticism of the old gossips in the village.

And so 'Isra and the young poor men of his age were the last 'brotherhood' and the old gossips whom the mayor didn't fear put their hopes on them. It was foolish, for the younger, uncircumcised brothers and sons of the 'brotherhood' were better for the village. They read and wrote and spoke English with the runner at the school as if it were their own language. But still the old men preferred 'Isra and his friends. And secretly they mistrusted the ponderous troupe of pupils who left with their pens and books for the school at eight each day.

Of the brotherhood 'Isra was their favourite, more popular than their own mayor's son who had gone away to colleges in England and Italy and got new wild ideas. They didn't need much excuse to like 'Isra. He was so easy. But when they retold how he had ridden his white mare that night of the rains across the hills to bring help for the mayor's chest, where his heart was beating and flapping like a trapped bird, they found all the excuse to like him thoroughly. The helicopter had come from the town on to the flat edge of the village and taken the mayor away to hospital. Four foreign doctors had slaved to quiet his heart and keep the mayorship with this old fearful man and away from the wild ideas of his wild college son. And 'Isra had returned to tell of his ride and that the chief would be well. Even the smallest children will say it. 'Isra-kone is the finest horseman in the valley.

'Isra was a quiet man, though a great talker when he chose, who had few certainties. He did not trust the weather or his cattle or the life of his horse whom he loved. When the weather was fine and his stock was healthy and he woke in the morning to find the horse bright-eyed and vigorous, then he let himself enjoy that day. But he did not expect it to hold for the next day. He expected only what he could see approaching with his own eye, and (since the

51

night darkness blocked his vision) his anticipations ended each day at sunset.

He had known, since the first swollen stomach of his boyhood, what it was to sit watchful at night beneath the stars. That was the extent of his mysticism. For the rest, he was happy while he had maize and fulfilled while he was popular in the village. In the two years since his ride across the mountains to bring the helicopter, he *had* allowed a small certainty into his life, that his comings and goings were commented on. That as he rode down from the lands the old men at the store nodded and smiled with affection and said, 'There's young 'Isra with his horse. What's he up to?' and called, 'Go well, 'Isra. Where are you riding?' Or, 'From where are you come?'

When the old men stopped calling and nodding and commenting they did not like him any less. It was just that their interests were elsewhere, fixed a little to the right of the wide erosion gulley on the ridge above the village where the teacher appeared each evening for an instant before disappearing and appearing again, jogging doggedly towards them and their gossip at the store.

'Isra watched his rival with the old men for a season until his own fame had eroded away and not even the men of his brotherhood turned to admire him and his white mare or whisper his name. Their eyes were not for one of their own whom they loved and trusted and understood but for the foreigner for whom they cared nothing, but who came faster and faster each day from the ridge below the sunset and who seemed to tell them something about man and their mountains which they had never guessed –

that men were like hares who could bounce across the black-studded basalt earth around which they had stumbled for centuries until the horse had come.

'Isra missed his fame for a season until he saw how he and his horse could regain it, bringing the attention of the villagers once again back to his entries and exits and his fine horsemanship and story-telling. Not planning ahead further than that day 'Isra timed the meeting with his rival for the evening.

He told old Loti. 'Me and the teacher are going to race tonight from the school to the store. Will you be there? Don't let anybody miss the race.'

Neither he nor old Loti nor the other gossips at the store doubted for an instant that 'Isra and his mare would beat the teacher. The horse was born to the mountains. But they looked forward to the contest. It would be interesting to see what the foreigner and his bony legs could do against the mountain and the horse.

The word soon spread through the village that 'Isra would race the teacher. But the last man to hear was the teacher himself. It was Sunday and the school was closed. He sat at the door of his house and ran his fingers across the ripple soles of his shoes. Still good. Good perhaps for another month or so . . . and then it wouldn't matter. His 'term' would be over and he would be back in Canada and running on track again. He'd need harder soles there. These ripples were good for the dry sloping hills which surrounded the school, for turning sharply on the thorny goat-ways and the rubble of the yearly erosion – but not for 'track'. Another month or so . . . and he'd have needed new running shoes, the thatch on the staff house would have to be replaced, new boys would be coming to the school. And he'd be in Montreal with his colour slides and a life-long commitment to this seventh and shabby continent, to the village in the next valley. Melvyn John Murphy was coming. His replacement. From Detroit, Michigan – motor city. He'd already written to the American and told him about the place, the school, the trick the sunlight had of flecking the aloes long after the light in the valleys had gone. He hoped that Melvyn John Murphy would respect the place like he had, would give what he had (though not quite as much) and take what was offered. They had their own ways, these people. Brashness would not be welcome.

He thought all this and decided that he would miss his running across the hills into the village. He decided, too, that he would preserve his sense of loss, even when his memory was faint and when his body and pace had got used once again to the flat white-lined cinder tracks and the soft spring-time training runs across the campus of Joliette College and along the lip of the river where girls sat with their bicycles on the grass. Somehow it was more noble and more worldly amongst the slipping soils and half-chewed thorns to pad pad pad along, nearly always dry, nearly always warm, always alone and with no competition, no other runners but yourself to run against.

He would preserve the loss of that.

The wind was dropping now as it did the hour before dusk. He pulled the ripples on and tied them tight and double so they would not loosen or snag on the low dry bushes. He turned his socks close down over his shoes so that his shins were exposed and could be cut on the sharp twigs and coarse grass of the track. It was good to scratch and draw blood in that safe place.

When he stood he saw 'Isra-kone standing next to his tough white mare at the edge of the school compound. Eddy Rivette walked over and greeted his visitor.

'Did you come to see me?'

'Isra nodded.

'What is it? To do with the school?'

'No, running. I want to race with you to the store.'

Eddy Rivette was half-pleased. It was good that one of the villagers should want to run with him, but this man was not dressed for running nor built for it. It was strange, that – for the man's decision to come to him at the school seemed firm and old but his appearance was that of a man who wanted to run on impulse, whatever he wore and despite his build.

'I go fast,' said Eddy discouragingly.

'My horse goes faster!'

'Your horse? You want to race me on your horse? Not running?'

'No, riding on my horse!'

They both laughed at the thought of 'Isra running. This was to be more of a contest because 'Isra was a fine rider and his horse was strong and used to the hills and the ways across them.

'Why do you want to run against me? Must the loser give something?'

'No,' said 'Isra. 'It is for the race only.'

'Okay. When?' asked Eddy.
'Now,' said 'Isra.

*

And that was how the Great Race between the schoolteacher and the horseman began – a simple challenge
brought to the school compound by a small uneasy man
with a horse to another small man, a runner from Canada.
Not a brother. Not a man from the villages amongst the
hills, but a stranger with a stranger's ways. 'When?' asked
the one. 'Now,' answered the other. And so the race
waited a few moments to begin, for the two men to
understand the race, that it was two different strengths
that were being matched.

'When you kick your horse I will start running,' said
Eddy Rivette. 'Isra nodded. 'It's the first to the store, is
that it?' 'Isra nodded again. 'We can go any way we want,
just get there first?'

'That's right,' said 'Isra.

'Let's go then!'

'Isra kicked his horse and turned the rein towards the
foot of the steep ridge which stood between him and the
crowd of villagers, his villagers, who waited at the ground
by the store. The horse speeded from a trot to a canter and
cut firmly and confidently into the slow gradient away
from the school. Eddy Rivette set off in pursuit, surprised
at the speed with which the horse was gaining ground. He
saw 'Isra choose the same cattle track which he himself had
used nightly for visits to the store. 'Isra had been watching

him, he realised. Any advantage that Eddy had from knowing the most economical route across the ridge was lost now that 'Isra had chosen it for himself. It would be impossible to pass, too, on that track. It was too narrow and its borders too treacherous for the delicate ankles of a man. Used to adapting his tactics to the dictates of the pack in the point-to-points and marathons that he had run in Canada, Eddy Rivette saw that the race was lost by his usual route. The horse had the advantage of speed on the flat and the advantage of being first and unpassable on the steep track. He would not be able to pass 'Isra until they reached the gentle gradient at the tree before the store and, by then, the horse's speed would make her the winner. He had to beat them on the hill or lose the race.

He made his mind up quickly, full-heartedly. When he reached the spot where the flatness of the school's half-valley turned abruptly upwards away from the loose stones and thorns into the erosions and cattle paths of the ridge, instead of following the horse and 'Isra, now sixty metres ahead and twenty metres above, Eddy Rivette turned at right angles. He paced out along the wide dry track, which rounded the foot of the ridge with scarcely a change of height before it reached the next valley, the valley of the village and the store. There it joined the broad sandy stream bed, the dead river of the valley, and climbed imperceptibly towards the single tree, the store and the waiting villagers. It was the long way round, perhaps twice the distance of the ridge route, but there wasn't an obstacle nor even a difficult stretch in the whole track. The obstacle was just one of distance. Eddy opened out his pace. It developed easily and his wind was with him. This was easy, plain sailing, after the difficulties that he had tamed daily on the cattle tracks of the ridge, the constant watching and skipping and allowing for hazards and the jarring of hard heels into an aching stomach, the creeping heartbeats waiting to pain him to a standstill. No, this was easy. He could forget those problems and just let his speed stretch with his step, his mind free to calculate the distance and tell himself again and again that it could not be done.

'Isra did not turn to look behind, to see the school-teacher running along the flat floor of the valley. It was bad luck to look behind. He fixed his eye on the summit of the ridge and rode happily, knowing that he was leading and that the schoolteacher, wherever he was, was behind. But he was careful not to tire his horse. She must be fresh enough to finish strongly, like a victor. 'Let the horse be slow enough to step firmly,' he told himself, 'but fast enough to arrive in time, like when I rode across the mountains to bring the helicopter to the mayor.' 'Isra reached the flat ledge of soily stone a few yards below the summit of the ridge where he had to turn the horse through a tight passage of rock to take the track to the top. The horse paused for a footing and 'Isra let himself glance at the track below. No sign of the teacher. Perhaps he was running in one of the deep gulleys and would appear in a moment. He listened. No, not a sound. He would have heard the slapping soles of the foreigner's shoes if he had been moving on that hillside, but not a sound and not a sign.

'Isra looked along the ridge to either side, fearing that

the teacher had taken a new, quicker route. Still no movement. 'Isra laughed. 'He is resting,' he said aloud, to the horse and the hills. 'He is tired and he is resting. We have won this race.' He spurred the horse up the last few metres of track and let himself enjoy both the pleasure of reaching the top and of having won midway through the race.

'He is resting,' he thought. 'Or perhaps he has fallen and is lying in the stones with his ankles twisted. We will send a horse to bring him down. *I* myself will ride to bring him down on the back of *my* horse.'

And when 'Isra, the rider of the village, reached the summit of the ridge he was laughing to himself.

At the village store old Loti and the villagers were waiting, their eyes crannied against the evening light silhouetting the hills before them. Loti and the old men knew which spot on the ridge to watch, the spot where the teacher had crossed each evening. They knew where the leader of the race would appear briefly before disappearing into the slip of an erosion gulley and then come in view again, lower down the hill where the track flattened. And though the villagers were watching the ridge too, it was their ears which were nervous, waiting for the old men to cry out 'Here he comes. It is . . .' and then the name of the man who led. They formed the two possible shapes on the still ridge, the runner or the horse, its tail frisky with victory.

And then Loti called, just one word, 'Isra, and they saw him there, the man of their village, winning on the ridge. A cry went up from the villagers, carrying across the evening to 'Isra. They saw him spur his horse and start to descend the track into the deep gulley, ferociously. 'He should stay calm,' the old men thought. 'He is in the lead.' But they did not know what 'Isra had seen jogging along the dry valley floor firmly and resolutely towards the village and the store. The schoolteacher had taken the long valley route and was running strongly on the obstacle-free road while he, 'Isra-kone, had still to take care amongst the treacherous descents, though he and his horse were nearer, much nearer, to the store.

'Isra's descent brought him to the valley track twenty metres ahead of the schoolteacher. He lost a metre only turning the horse on to it and urging her to the new course. But the last scrambled descent from the ridge after 'Isra had spotted the schoolteacher had unnerved her and she settled badly. Eddy Rivette, however, had not changed his pace. He had kept his steady step from the moment that he had decided not to challenge 'Isra on the ridge route but follow the contours of the valley. His steadiness kept him behind the horse and he knew from experience that the race depended on the sprint. But when and how? A fast one now to take the lead and keep it with stamina? Or leave it till the end and take it at the post? Or split it in two? Two half sprints – the first to worry the horse and the rider, the second to pass them. Yes, by far the best tactic and the safest one, not taking things too early or leaving them too late. Eddy Rivette went forward on his toes and opened his pace. He closed the gap between him and the horse but it had tired him and he was glad to tuck in behind

'Isra and let the animal do the work for the fifty metres before the final bend at the single tree towards the store. He had meant it as half his sprint but he realised that he had no more race in him, that that sprint was all that was left and that now, at best, he could hang on behind the horse, drawn in to her flanks, and come in level at least with the horse's tail though a saddle's length behind 'Isra.

Eddy Rivette knew the race for him was lost, but 'Isra did not know it was won. The sight of the schoolteacher easing across the flat valley had worried him but he had thought he was safe when he reached the track, ahead. But the schoolteacher had closed *that* gap in moments and with the speed of a young dog and was pressing him close, running at the horse's speed and drawing tighter and tighter into the movement of the mare. They must go faster, faster, before the teacher ran like that again and ate up the metres and 'Isra's fame in the village. His knees were sharp in the horse's side and his toes were fierce. Go horse, he said, go go. And he was fierce with the white mare, nagging her across those last few metres. The schoolteacher, with hardly a breath finding space in his lungs, hung on in the wake of warm air between the animal and its dust.

And then Eddy Rivette heard something new: a rasp in the horse's lungs that told him 'Isra was driving her too harshly and that, maybe, if only he could stay the pace of that gallop, the horse would have to slow sometime.

Both men heard both lungs racking, the runner and the horse both wanting the race over so that they could halt the pounding and gasp in air and air and normalise their hearts and lungs and shocked legs. No distance now. Just the turn and the few metres to the villagers at the store.

Eddy Rivette's lungs gave. He slowed and stooped a little, his hand on his chest below his heart, the pain building up, the horse moving ahead. He would finish. He was professional enough to finish and he was strong enough to recover quickly. But he would finish last, second to 'Isra and his horse, and that good race would be run.

Horse and 'Isra were at the last bend, taking it with panic and joy, not sure but sure enough that in a moment there would be cheers and the cheers would be theirs. 'Isra glimpsed the flagging schoolteacher a metre and a half behind, half caught up in the hoof dust. He leant with his horse into the bend at the tree and urged her into it, leaning far out like a yachtsman as pivot to the bend. The white mare was upright and tired, taking the turn as best she could. She felt her rider's weight shift towards the tree and went with it, too tired to resist. Her body came down. Her feet went away. She hit the dust of the track with her shoulder, the rest of her body bunched behind, hoofing the air, and sliding for a moment, doing the real damage to her tired white shoulder and to the man's thin leg on which she had fallen.

Not a whinny from her, too tired and breathless. Not a cry from 'Isra, too shamed already. One small gasp from the teacher, a cry of victory suppressed through experience until the line was crossed. A great whoop from the villagers, from the cackle of Loti to the yelp of the schoolchildren, as the winner of the race crossed the line of shadow marked at the side of the store by a low and sinking sun.

*Four*

# On Heat

## I

Once a year, at high tide on the longest day, the tiger crabs come ashore to mate. They come in their millions, as docile and purposeful as pilgrims. Nowadays the solstice is a national holiday and the coast is swarming with people, too. They inspect the striped and shifting shingle of the beach and lift the plumpest crabs for the pot.

But when we were young the beach was free and empty. We helped my father with his plate camera. We collected swabs of sperm. We measured carapaces and pincers. We marked the shells of specimens in indelible ink. Father introduced us as his 'young research assistants' whenever the kelp-farmers or the fishermen paused to stare. His book was published in 1928 and, thereafter, we stopped coming to the solstice beach. He was too busy at the Institute and travelling abroad. But we were mentioned in the preface and thanked for our 'tireless field work' – and the new edition carries a photograph of the family, taken in 1926. My two younger sisters, fat and cheerful, are shaking crabs at the camera. My mother, dressed from throat to ankle in a then-fashionable bandok, is sitting cross-legged in the centre of our lunch rug. A book in her lap. A look of explosive irritation on her face. My father, his head turned against the wind, his eyes narrowed,.is pointing at the camera and shouting instructions to the enlisted fisherman on how to focus and what to press. I am standing at father's side – an awkward, bony twelve-year-old in a torn and spermy dress. Before and beyond us, reduced to stones by this still, black-and-white photograph, are the tiger crabs. *Uca felix*, father called them. Lucky crabs. Free from the tyrannies of courtship and concupiscence.

'What is the mechanism which causes *Uca felix* to mate *en masse* on this single day?' asks father in the foreword to *The Secret Life of the Tiger Crab*. 'What is the chemistry of its procreative regularity?' His book does not provide the answers. Its popular appeal lay in the final chapters where father contrasted the rigid breeding behaviour of the crab with the uneven profligacy of human kind. Nature is always patterned, he said. It was his theory – and regret –

that the sexual life of *Homo sapiens* functioned in a state of disorder, 'outside of nature'.

*

My father died in 1940. My mother, in a gesture which was both ironic and dutiful, buried him in a weighted casket just above the high-tide mark and planted a salt bush to mark the spot. The Institute put up a raised stone tablet with an inscription:

PROFESSOR T. D. ZOEA

1879–1940

Writer and Natural Scientist

There is a photograph of this, too, at the back of the new edition.

*

A third photograph was not included, despite its combative prominence in my father's study. How he loved that photograph and how we feared it. Its date was 1912. My mother and father stood like big game hunters, striking poses for the long exposure of the filmplate in the darkness of the trees. All around them, blurred by impatience and playfulness, were a host of forest women, their arms latticed with cicatrices, their stomachs bulbous, their hilarity bombarding the grimness of my parents. 'All

69

Pregnant and Correct' was my father's title for the photograph. But my mother – and we three girls in our turn – found the laughing herd of women, their polished breasts and stomachs crowding the frame, oppressive.

'That was taken during the expedition,' my mother explained in those weeks when her illness made her reckless. 'The Professor and I had just married. I liked him enough to travel with him in those days. We rode on donkeys for eight weeks from the railhead at Etar. He was noting species and I was logging them for him in the yellow ledger. I wrote "Two donkeys" at the head of each day's list, and then the names that he called to me whenever there was movement in the undergrowth. It was as if we were not married, but still teacher and doting student . . . except that the Professor wanted sexual conjunction all the time, on the thinnest of pretexts. The moment we dismounted from our donkeys for rest or food the Professor would become attentive in that breathless, urgent way which so transformed him and so reduced him.'

We drew from her a portrait of my father made tense and engrossed by my mother's presence, as if his self-control had been agitated by the bounce of the donkey. At night in their tent, with the moth lamp burning and the camp flaps shaking a beat, he would again go to her, saying, 'Let me warm you' or 'You are beautiful in this light' or 'Hold me there.' At his most wheedling, his speech would be, 'Tonight I am tired. Take it in your hand and rub me to sleep.' At his boldest, he briefly left the tent and returned like some foolish stranger to push money into her hand and say, 'Be a whore for me. Pull up your nightclothes.' Sometimes there would be tears of shame, too. But for them the only remedy was more conjunction. 'Now we are married we can make love,' he told her, 'at any time.' 'Like animals,' she said, meaning to tease him but also, perhaps, to induce a little forbearance and composure when next his tumescence demanded her attention. 'No, not like animals,' he said. 'The very opposite to animals with their seasons, their ruts, their "heats", slaves to chemistry. No, it is this which separates us from the animals, our capacity to enjoy our bodies as the whim takes us, ever receptive to pleasure. Any place, any time. Now, for instance?'

\*

'In the eighth week we came deep into the forest where the people had made clearings for plantation,' said mother. 'The villagers there were naked by day and the Professor was much charmed by their innocence. He took notes, of course, as if the villagers were bats or beetles, and he was struck by the absence of sexual playfulness or arousal. "They are immodest like infants", he wrote in the ledger. But all our observations seemed inconsequential once the villagers had become used to our presence and their women felt free to go about their business. As you can see from the photograph, all of them except the children and the elderly were pregnant. Not surprising, perhaps, in a society where there were few constraints on fertility. But look closely at the women. Here is the oddity which so engaged the Professor. All these women are over eight months pregnant and they are ready to produce offspring in near unison.'

This observation set my father's mind racing. Birth in unison indicated conception in unison, the impregnation of the village's fertile women in one concentrated period of communal – if not public – sexual intercourse. What could be the purpose of such a congress? And were the mechanisms of its control social or biological? 'The Professor, to my cost, found the subject stimulating in every way,' complained mother. 'But there were lessons there for me also. I determined that the moment we returned to the city I would take charge of our conjugal lives. We would economise.'

\*

Now consider this. A trapper from the valley whom my father employed to transport his specimens and supplies to and from Etar, claimed to understand a little 'forest', a tongue so labio-plosive that linguists had titled it vabap-vabap. To hear it spoken in jostling conversation was to hear a flock of doves take wing. The trapper had been hunting amongst these same trees four years previously. And he had witnessed – had, indeed, participated in – a period of communal sexual intercourse amongst the small forest community with whom my parents were now lodged. 'You imagine them to be simple and cold,' he said, recounting his many previous attempts to find or buy a partner amongst the native women. 'Love-making does not interest them, it seems. But when their moment comes they are like dogs in heat.' I will not recount the scenes which he described or comment, either, on the opportunism of the trapper. After three days their sexual agitation, however, was reported to have ceased as readily and as inexplicably as it had begun. 'And the women with whom you had consorted?' asked my father. 'How many women . . . personally, may I ask . . . in those three days?' The man's reply is marked in my father's ledger and heavily circled. 'Fourteen!'

'The Professor's interest in the unrecorded smaller species in which the forest abounded was abandoned,' said mother. 'He postponed our return home for a further six weeks. He was determined to witness the communal birth for himself. I was left relatively unpestered in the charge of a girl whom the Professor nicknamed Puppy, because she could pronounce the word. She was, perhaps, a month or so too young for pregnancy, poor thing. She was quite happy to collect and cook our food and, indeed, to wear the dresses which I loaned her. I could not have her naked at our table. I taught her cat's cradle and hopscotch. It was foolish, perhaps. But she was sweet – an awkward, bony little thing – and I was bored beyond endurance. I had no tasks, and though the Professor and his trapper were huddled in conversation and much laughter until late at night, I was excluded. Except from Puppy.'

In the meantime – and with the trapper's vabap-vabap at his shoulder – my father busied himself with monitoring the pregnancies and with keeping a journal. 'We start with the notion of menstrual synchrony,' he wrote. 'It is well established amongst the women of even the most civilised households throughout the world. The monthly cycles of women in close and regular physical proximity harmonise and correspond. They run in parallel. They ovulate simultaneously. The aetiology of such a phenomenon is not established, though olfactory and glandular agencies are most likely. Nature is neither wasteful nor gratuitous. The mechanism for reproductive synchrony is latent in humankind. We must take this as evidence that such a mechanism was at one time fully active as confidently as we must presume an ancient tail implicit in our own vestigial coccyx or a full pelt of hair as ancestral to those few strategic tufts which still endure. Any synchrony of sexual intercourse, pregnancy and birth amongst the forest people, a community otherwise free of profligacy or baser passions, suggests a practice too fettered and precise to bear an anthropological interpretation of custom or taboo. Here, cut off from humankind for centuries beyond number, is a species whose reproductive natures are as different from our own as a gibbon's from a chimp's. Are we to witness a mass human parturition as brief and ordered in duration as that observed by shepherds amongst their sheep? Is this the natural, primitive pattern of human reproduction from which our own sexual connivance has evolved and which was thought lost amongst the orchards of what the Christians label Eden?'

*

'It was a wearying experience,' said mother. 'As you

would expect, the men made all the noise, with their own backache and sickness and their stomachs distended with phantom offspring. The women were silent and out of sight, of course.' Her recollections were bitter and, perhaps, distorted too. She described a village barmy with pregnancy. And then one morning the men went off into the forest to give mimed birth to the stones which they decorated or to the wooden dolls which they had carved. And in the shelters of the village the first curious skirlings of the babies began. It was an orphan chorus of human gulls, she said, the clutter rather than the mystery of birth. 'The Professor, of course, was not welcome at that time with his calipers, camera and notebook. Nor would they accept assistance from me, though my presence, with Puppy at my side, was at least ignored. The births themselves seemed relatively easy; labour was short – as if the stones and dolls now produced by their men had freed the women from a punishing confinement. Or so your father said. For myself I have never discovered the attraction of small babies. And here were two hundred or so, pupped like seals within three days.'

How many survived? How many bore healthy offspring? Some were stillborn, cordulated or drowned. Others perished within minutes or hours or days. The unlucky mothers – children some of them, a month or so older than Puppy; in a kinder world they would have been schoolgirls – ruptured or haemorrhaged. For some the placenta tore and there was bleeding, pain and slow death. But for every bereaved mother there was an orphan child to suckle. 'Left to its own devices, nature is cruel but tidy,' my father noted. And once the men had returned and the waste had been buried and the dead separated from the living, the forest people went back to their business, as gentle and as calm and as casual as sheep without rams.

My father whispered his proposition to mother in the darkness of their bedding – that they had encountered humankind in its sexual infancy, that the forest people were specialists in the brief encounter, like that observed amongst bullfrogs, hammer-headed bats, kakopo parrots and the mass aerial dance of mosquitoes. And, of course, his dreadful legions of tiger crabs. 'Where is the evidence?' my mother asked him, dutifully displaying the cynicism on which he as her teacher had insisted. 'All you have is a host of shared birthdays and the four-year-old gossip of a trapper. His testimony might not impress a scientific seminar in quite the way you hope.' 'We will gather evidence,' he said. 'How?' My father patiently listed the rituals and procedures of scientific field study to his bride, his student. 'And for this, of course,' he said, 'a cadaver is required.'

In his journal, he wrote: 'The estrus cycle or period of "heat" during which female mammals are receptive to males is, if Elgie's work is to be accepted at face value, controlled by the ovarian cocoon. Follicles secrete a natural scent to advertise readiness and availability and, also, to trigger a sexual response in the males. Is this the secret of the forest women, simply an enlarged cocoon inactive, except occasionally and communally, once a year or less? Are the odours of chemistry still as eloquent here as amongst bears and antelope, while we – our estrus lost as surely as our tails – enjoy our tamed and liberated embraces, triggered by our hearts and not our tyrant vesicles, free and equal, donors and recipients of physical affection?

'What of their men? It is evident that the testes of the forest males are considerably enlarged. Measurements of my own testes and those of the reluctant trapper, who is now employed as my assistant and interpreter, compare unfavourably with those of the two young males who quite amicably allowed us to take calipers to their private parts. I estimate a size difference in an approximate ratio of five to three. What can be the function of the larger testicle other than the enhanced production of sperm and the increased power of impregnation necessary for the precise and efficient service of females who are sexually receptive for a short period only? I become more convinced that my hypotheses will sustain closer scientific analysis. If I were dealing with one of the lower primates, I would instruct my trapper to shoot some specimens. The matters of genital volume and weight, of sacs, cocoons and vesicles, could then be readily established with scalpel and scales. But here we are dealing with human kind – in almost every detail of surface anatomy, proportion and pigmentation identical to myself and my dear wife. But what are the subcutaneous secrets of these people? Only surgery and autopsy can provide the answers. What will the knife reveal?'

\*

The trapper's 'forest' was not equal to the task. He could flap his plosives in simple barter or requests for food. But no words, he said, in this or any language were adequate for what my father was now demanding. Sixteen women, a dozen or so foetuses, had died in birth. Their bodies were lying in a shelter under damp leaves. Soon, unless they were burned or buried, their flesh would putrefy, provide nesting sites for swag-flies or lunch for termites. 'Tell them I want one female adult,' said father. 'And a male infant. And a male of reproductive age, if at all possible. I'll pay. Can you explain the urgency, that flesh rots, that I am a scientist, a wise man?'

The trapper did his best and devised a sentence. 'Scientist' he could not translate. But he knew the word for Magician. 'Body' became Meat. 'This man big magician,' he said, pointing at my father who stood with a fixed smile on his face and his mediocre genitals well hidden by his fieldwork trousers. 'You give magician meat of one woman, one man, one boy. Dead meat from that house, very quick.' He pointed at the shelter where the victims of childbirth had been placed. Those few of the men who could understand the trapper's words shook their heads, not in anger but in puzzlement. The man-who-pincers-testicles is a man-eater, too, they told their comrades. The information seemed to cause hilarity rather than anger. 'What are they saying?' asked my father. 'They think you are a cannibal,' said the trapper. 'You want dead bodies – what else could you be?'

'We packed up for departure speedily then,' said my mother. 'The Professor feared that we had outstayed our welcome, that the people would take against us.' But he and the trapper were conspiring. A cadaver which could not be bought, they reasoned, could be stolen. They could camp a safe distance from the village and then return at night with a donkey and some ropes. Three bodies was too ambitious, clearly. But the body of one of the mothers would provide useful data . . . and would perhaps not be missed from beneath those damp leaves.

'They wished to spare my feelings,' she said. 'The Professor told me that they would spend the night trapping the bat-moths which were conspicuous in those parts. He and the trapper – did we never learn his name? – went off at dusk with a donkey and a rifle and, I must presume, circled our camp-site until they had regained the path to the village. How could I guess their true purpose? I slept, glad to be free of squalling infants and the attentions of the Professor who, even after his erection had been reduced, would nightly sleep against my back as if I were a child's bolster. We were camped at the edge of the trees and there were few sounds except the snapping of the donkey halters and the occasional owl. I dreamed, too. Something sweet and domestic and kindly, with my sister and our mother brought back from the dead – all of us eating and me singing and that house of wood with its cool flapping screens.'

And then – that cliché – a dry twig snapped in the trees followed by the silence of held breath. It could have been an owl, roosting carelessly on bad wood, or a bell nut splitting and showering its seed. But it woke my mother as sharply as a gun shot. As far as she could see in the darkness, with the moon behind the trees and her eyes still startled by sleep, the donkey, the equipment, the specimen boxes, the dry rations were still where my father had left them. She imagined a thief or villager cutting loose a donkey. Or a scrub dog snouting for food. It seemed safer to leave the tent and crouch by the donkey. She walked the few yards in bare feet, taking with her an iron pot which she could beat on a stone if there were animals to scare off. Then a timid dove took wing as a small voice spoke to her from the darkness and a figure moved out of the trees towards the camp, still talking, 'Viper-biper-parb . . .' 'Who is it?' mother said. But she knew. The girl, Puppy, had come.

\*

My father's journal is silent on the events of that evening. These are the possibilities. Perhaps by the time he and the trapper reached the village, the dead were already buried. They found the site of recent digging but, as their only equipment was a length of rope, a lantern and a moth net, what could they do? Or, perhaps, the forest people lay in wait. They had expected my father to return. They chased him off. Or my father took fright. Half-way through the trees, startled by a cracking twig as Puppy, maybe, passed them in the dark, he and the trapper lost their taste for body snatching. Or they reached the shelter of the dead and pulling back the leaves they found stench and rankness. The termites and the swag-flies had been at work.

But when my father returned without so much as a single bat-moth, his mood of irritation was soon replaced by a vivaciousness which my mother could not trust or understand. She and Puppy sat cross-legged in the shade like tailors as my father and the trapper concocted their tale of misfortune, of moths evading their net, of opportunities thwarted by undergrowth too thick for the night-time lepidopterist. 'And why is she here?' asked father, pointing at the girl. In reply Puppy herself pointed out across the plain towards Etar. 'She followed me,' said mother. 'She wants to come with us. She thinks it's paradise out there. She wants a dress like mine. It's all impossible. You'll have to take her back.' My father disagreed; he couldn't go back, he said. He wasn't welcome. 'Then what'll you do?' asked mother. 'Leave her here? She's little more than a child. What is she, twelve, thirteen?' 'She can come with us,' said father. 'You'll need some help around the house. You've said you like her.' It was, according to mother, little better than kidnapping, slavery. But father was determined. If they left, the girl would follow, he said. She was like a stray puppy – yes, the nickname had been apposite – which had found a warm home. She wanted to come. She was an adult almost, no matter how tiny her breasts and narrow her hips. She was a free individual. This was her chance to make something of her life. Let her come. Make her welcome.

★

## II

My mother slept, while my sisters and I, made self-conscious and dutiful by her illness (her madness) aired and tidied the house, polished the cluttered sapwood tables of the reception rooms, threw out old papers, dry plants and bad food. And (as if she was already a corpse) we opened her unanswered mail, checked the contents of the family box which she kept beneath the bed, and leafed through the albums of cards and photographs.

'She's remarkably strong for a woman in her nineties,' the doctor said. 'Her heart and lungs are good, but her mind has gone.' She was cogent, it seemed, but cantankerous, and meddlesome. That is why we had been summoned. She had thrown soup at the night-nurse. Her 'things' went missing, she said, and everybody – the doctor, the neighbours, old friends – had been accused of theft. She spat out her pills. She lived in the past. Which of us, the doctor asked, had room enough and time and patience to offer mother a home. 'We're none of us young,' I said. 'I'm seventy-two. My heart and lungs aren't strong, not like mother's. I smoke. We all smoke.' The doctor shrugged. He'd done his duty. It was up to us to sort it out.

It was over cigarettes that we discovered a photograph which none of us had seen before. I pulled it from a brittle envelope amongst the monographs and dissertations which our mother had preserved from my father's archives. A pale triangle cornered the photograph where seventy years of sunlight had blanched the print. Its year was 1914, the year of my own birth. My father, looking older than his thirty-five years in a half-beard, was seated on the veranda at a table – the one that now stood in the corner of mother's room, heavy with medicines. My mother – a little blurred – was standing at his side, dramatically cutting slices of gourd for the guests and for the camera. We could recognise one or two of the faces, younger versions of the remote professors and their wives who worked with my father at the Institute and who had ignored us when we were children. We recognised crockery, too, and the chairs, and the white heads of the fessandra bushes where then – and still – the cats took their refuge. The 'kidnapped' maid who stood in the sunlight at the edge of the veranda, half-turned and smiling like the guests into the camera, was – as mother had described her – tiny, sweet and thirteen. She wore service gloves and a white cotton dress. An empty tray hung by her side. Her feet were bare. Of all the people there she seemed the least self-conscious, attempting to present nothing of herself except the smile. 'Well, she looked happy enough,' I said.

But other papers in my father's handwriting made me wonder. He noted her listlessness during the early days of their return from the forests, her reluctance to stay for long inside the house, the chaos of her digestive system as she encountered city foods for the first time. She lost weight. Her face, pert and cheerful by nature, thinned and paled. 'The Professor took measurements, of course. What else? Her height, her cranial circumference, her daily temperature,' said mother, awake and garrulous again with the photograph of the veranda party in her hand. 'But he did not consult doctors. Doctors have colleagues. They gossip. Can you imagine the rapacity of these men, the anthropologists, the quacks, the weather cocks, the dilettantes, the journalists, the tuft-hunters, if under the cloak of science they could attend the village of the mating tribe. Communal intercourse, global mayhem. No, your father wanted Puppy, all to himself. "She's our secret," he said. And so to our friends and the neighbours, she was just another country girl, none too bright, illiterate, clumsy, compliant. The men adored her.'

But my father, she said, seemed unmoved by Puppy's innocence and charm. For him she was briefly, each morning, an object of scientific scrutiny, and then forgotten. Eventually the girl would be returned to her home, the village in the forest. But first he wished to monitor and chart her cycles. His charts survive amongst his papers – two columns of figures with dates relating to . . . two women? Only by standing amongst the cabinets and desks of what had been my father's study could I construct from these numbers and chemical abbreviations a picture of my father in research. His daily readings measured the presence and absence of vaginal acids secreted during ovulation and that period of sexual excitement titled estrus amongst the lower mammals. The first column – Puppy's? – recorded unbroken torpor. The second – my mother's? – showed a conventional monthly cycle, the acids increasing towards the middle of the cycle and then decreasing.

Was this, then, the household ritual? Breakfast served and eaten. My father in his study coat, my mother in her morning clothes, Puppy in that white cotton dress and those incongruous gloves. The couch in the corner of the study. Sterilised bottles, cotton swabs. The forest girl, for reasons she could not quite guess but which she could have taken as some odd city custom, required to lie back and raise her knees while my father conducted his inspection and made his notes. And then my mother's turn, her mistress, her hop-scotch pal, submitting in the same room at the same time to reassure the girl that all was normal.

Once more, from mother, we heard her portrait of my father sharp-set and pestering in her presence, particularly on those days when swabs revealed her to be chemically receptive. 'He'd been a studious bachelor for too long,' she said. 'Through me he was catching up on all those lost liaisons which should have occupied his youth instead of skeletons and dried skins and bird's eggs. But I was not so foolish as I had been on our forest expedition. Look at his charts. You'll see what games I played.' Indeed, within four months of Puppy's arrival the acid levels of my mother's discharge in the ovulation stages of her monthly cycle halved, then quartered, and then (by the seventh month) disappeared entirely. 'The Professor was perplexed,' she said. 'His appetites, poor man, were no longer justified by scientific data. He became less troublesome.'

In his journal, father wrote: 'An unexpected development. My wife who has acted as a conventional control against whom I am able to verify the results of my experiments with P. continues to menstruate in a more or less regular pattern but her vaginal secretions of oliphatic acids have ceased. Her estrus levels now synchronise with those of P., unchanging from day to day, with no peaks or troughs to indicate sexual and reproductive readiness or periods of non-fertility. The two women now chemically harmonise and correspond in their sexual inertia. Here we observe the fact if not the mechanism of reproductive synchrony. Modern sexual licence comes into line with the more ordered ways of simpler times.' 'He was a fool,' said mother, 'and careless. I douched myself with potash soap in those days when my acids were expected. His swabs were worthless.'

Except, that is, when in the fourteenth month, the daily swab taken from Puppy indicated a slight rise in its acid levels. My father took more swabs. He repeated the analysis. His findings were identical. My mother's own secretions – the charts are here to prove it – showed no increased acidity on that or subsequent days. But, on the second day, Puppy's small breasts were swollen, her cheeks were hot, the glands in her throat and armpits had hardened, her genitals had darkened. And her acids had doubled in strength. 'This is it,' said father, now hot and overwrought himself. 'She's in heat.' 'Good, good, good,' he said to Puppy. 'You will be famous.' She smiled at the repeated words and at my father's unusual turbulence, his breathlessness, his solicitude as he sat her at the chair of his desk and drew from its drawer .his thermometer and his stethoscope and his speculum. My mother closed the door upon them and went to read and sleep elsewhere in the house.

*

And that is the end of the story. Except for two columns of

figures with dates, an entry or so in my father's journal, a small figure in a single photograph, the cantankerous memories of a nonagenarian (whose loquacity stops there, at the closed door of my father's study), where is the evidence that this girl, this Puppy, followed my parents' donkeys from the forests to the city, that she lived in this creaking house, serving at the table and on the study couch? Search, if you will, amongst the papers and paraphernalia of the Zoea archive at the Institute. Nine hundred items from lecture notes on elephant musts and the monogamous gibbon to the manuscript of *The Secret Life of the Tiger Crab* chart my father's lifelong reconnaissance of breeding chemistry and behaviour. Yet where are those people of the forests? And where is Puppy and those days of swabs and patience? My mother could not say. She soon forgot the conversations which had sustained us in the early phases of her illness. And once my sisters had returned to their families and left me, the spinster, here alone to cope, my mother would speak only of more recent years, the money that my father's book brought in, the thankful respites of his trips abroad, his burial on the beach with the wind and the distinguished mourners and the bouncing of the shingle as it fell upon his casket throughout the weeping and the obituaries. She had been a widow a long time, she said, and she had no continuous memories of my father now, just snapshots from the family album.

While mother slept, I sat at my father's desk with those three disquieting snapshots – the beach, the women, the veranda – and searched for a better ending to my mother's story. His journal spoke of his 'dear wife', his 'loyal companion in research', 'the angel who is mother to my girls'. But, otherwise, the notes were obsessively academic and dry. His dedication to the natural sciences seemed unbroken, humourless, without restraint. 'I have been asked to prepare a pamphlet on the forest phenomenon,' he wrote finally in his diary for 1926, 'but I am not happy to proceed. It seems to me that the evidence is thin and that the absence for a year or more of menstruation and estrus in P. was possibly contingent on late puberty or the disruptions of weight loss, anxiety and digestive complications brought about by her hasty relocation in the town. Moreover, travellers from the Institute have not been able to establish the whereabouts of P.'s village. The plantation has been abandoned and, no doubt, her people have either descended like so many others to work on farms or to offer themselves in service in the towns, or they have withdrawn further into the trees, where, perhaps, it would be a kindness to leave them. At some later time all this would warrant an amusing memoire of conclusions rashly reached by a natural scientist too eager and ambitious. I smile at my younger self, but, for the moment, *Uca felix* calls and we – my wife, my three girls – are repairing to the coast.' And nothing more.

I stood before the peeling mirror on the wall of his study and smiled at my older self. Thin and dry and squeamish. I looked again at that family photograph and wondered at the girl encountered there, in her torn and spermy dress, the slight and bony exception of the beach. My mother and my sisters were broad and tall with heavy hips and wide-set, comfortable eyes. Even the *Uca felix* were wide and swollen for the solstice.

Then the bulbous women and the girl in the cotton dress and the service gloves, that slight, pale teenager with the empty tray and the smile and the fessandra blooms, looked out at me from the other fading prints. Who – in my position, with my dismay – would not hurry now to unearth those charts again, to match her dates and mine, to sit lifeless in that chair (where she had sat, her face flushed, her breasts swollen, her acids flowing), to shut both eyes and hear those doves take wing, vabap-vabap, the shingle and the crabs, the baying of the donkeys left alone and tethered in the ardour of the night, the closing of a study door?

*Five*

# Sins and Virtues

I used once to have a calligrapher's booth in the market place. Bridegrooms came and I blessed their marriage certificates with the name of God in gold-leaf. I provided decorative alphabets for elementary schools and delicate pillow-prayers on silk for the superstitious. The old came to my booth and detailed their sins and virtues. I inscribed them into a list on parchment soaked in ambergris and sealed them into a tube of bamboo. So when the old were dead, their Sins and Virtues were burned with them.

I was the only calligrapher in the city who possessed the

franchise to profit from Sins and Virtues. It provided great business but precluded me from marriage and fornication. That was the custom and the regulation. The sin-lister must be free from sin.

Later, when business superseded religion as the pre-occupation of our people, I decorated shop fronts and designed letterheads for ambitious greengrocers and ice-vendors. I prepared boastful posters for the first cinema, ornamental scrolls for lofty institutions and fancy gate-plates for embassies. My work on parchment was etched and woven and carved into more durable materials by craftsmen in Europe. I extended my booth and employed an apprentice to mix my inks and to deliver my work. But that was long ago. Now I am nearly dead. The acacia which my uncles planted in their village at my birth (its name in Siddilic signifies 'Patience') has almost lost its leaves. Only one branch draws sap. The rest is the home of ants.

*

I do not now go into the market. I spend my days almost entirely within the walls of this echoing and lizard-infested house. I start work each day at my Morning Desk, which faces eastwards towards the river. At noon I dine on some delicacy – a modest snack of grilled perch or, when they are seasonable, locusts. I no longer eat red meat or drink wine. My head and my stomach are too vulnerable. A little honey water is sufficient. Or some sweet mint tea. I sleep for an hour or so beneath my one fan. My house gecko joins me, lying across my bare chest like a damp medallion.

In the afternoon I move to my Afternoon Desk, facing into the sun of the courtyard and the evergreen of the oleander. I burn a stick of fine cinnamon to keep the devils at bay. An old habit. I work until moonrise and then eat again: some tomatoes or beans with a little sour bread, followed by a mango or guava or a fruit milk-shake from the machine at the shop on the corner. I change my white day clothes – now soiled with pips and juice and crumbs – and put on heavier evening wear for my third work shift at the Evening Desk in the inner room. If I want some ink, perhaps, or some small delicacy, then I send Sabino, who was my boy apprentice and is now my factotum, to the market and to the new air-conditioned stores.

I myself have withdrawn from the market place. I am now too grand for marriage certificates and shop fronts and lofty institutions. What I did for the price of an olive in my youth I will not now consider even for an orchard of olive trees. I have made my small fortune and, in what time there is left, I am looking for inner meanings. I am the last and certainly the most distinguished of calligraphers in the old Siddilic script but I am done with weaving and ennobling letters, of chasing their edges into the corner of the page. Now I am a doodler. Every leaf of gold-foil counts for me as an acacia leaf. I am in no hurry to use up my supply. I work three shifts from habit, from boredom and to exercise the arthritis in my hands. My mind is elsewhere, searching out material for my last work, to be burned at my funeral.

*

They call my craft Art these days and pay great sums for it. Last month a collector from Chicago offered Duni the ironmonger three thousand dollars for his ancient shop front with my flaking age-old letters. I went down to the market place on Sabino's arm to witness the dismantling.

'We'll take great care of it, sir,' the American told me, cracking my frail hands between his own. 'We're going to restore it, right? We're going to give it a fresh lick of paint and we're going to put it on show in the Museum of Ethnography. The people of America will be able to see your work. Back home, artists and historians are just beginning to appreciate the subtleties of Siddilic. This is such a beautiful piece.' He stood back and admired Duni's shop front. 'Wonderful,' he said. 'Sir, I am proud to be acquainted with you.'

Three thousand dollars! Duni had paid me for the work with cooking pots. 'DUNI EMPIRE', I had written on his instruction, 'POTS, TOOLS, SEEDS, BICYCLES AT FAVOURABLE PRICES. TOILET SUPPLIES.' I pray for the people of Chicago.

*

Word has spread that Americans are buying up shop fronts. Enterprising businessmen have purchased them and are storing them for museums and universities abroad. Old ladies have been digging in their treasure trunks for old marriage certificates marked in gold by my brush. Embassies have placed guards on their gate-plates. The cinema manager is cursing his lack of foresight.

Back-street charlatans have turned their energies from pimping and fortune-telling to forgery. The market is full of false shop fronts: fake greengrocers, tinkered tailors.

Visitors from America and Europe can buy mass-produced pillow-prayers in warped and clumsy Siddilic. In the market place, as in Chicago, the ancient characters of Siddilic have lost their meaning. The only care the forgers take is with my signature and, because their hands are young, these signatures are now better than my own.

Sabino is growing rich on the pickings from my waste-basket. Dollars cannot tell doodles from the name of God.

*

There has been some excitement in my small street. A government minister has come expressly to see me. First of his entourage to arrive was his head of protocol, a young gum-chewing aide-de-camp. He was a stickler for procedure. First, he distributed with a sweep of his arm a handful of coins to the beggars and children of our quarter. He shook some hands. He kicked some backsides. Nothing was too much trouble for him. He would be back in twenty minutes, he explained, with the Minister and with more handfuls of cash. Ministerial protocol demanded an eager crowd.

I was taking my siesta. 'Do not wake your employer,' he instructed Sabino. 'The Minister likes surprises. But tidy the house.' He placed one of his men outside the front gate to my house and another in the back yard. Then he radioed from his army jeep that the street was now ready for the Minister's casual arrival. I slept peacefully and dreamt of my booth.

Sabino conducted the Minister into my room. I woke to their whisperings and shufflings and the scrape of the proffered chairs. But I kept still and listened. The Minister sat, chewing some of his aide's gum, and waited for me to stir. My gecko backed furtively up my chest towards my throat. The Minister was a patient man. He enjoyed the advantage of arriving unannounced and being kept waiting.

I tired quickly of dissembling. I opened an eye – quite an effort for an old man long past winking – and focused first on my gecko, then my toes with their fossilised toenails, and finally the Minister. Our smiles were hollow.

'No, no, please don't get up,' he said. 'We can talk here.' He watched my white lizard, now shuffling squat-legged down my stomach towards the dark safety of the bed sheet which draped my legs and loins.

'You live modestly for such a wealthy man,' he said at last.

'Wealthy?'

'A millionaire by now, I should say.'

I said nothing. The Minister was talking monkey-shine.

'You have been selling your work abroad at great profit.' He took from the inner pocket of his handmade suit a thick wad of paper and tossed it on to the bed.

'Evidence,' he said. 'There is an article about you in the *New York Times* by a man who spent many thousands of dollars on your shop signs and pillow-prayers. There is a list there of over a hundred foreigners who have paid great sums for your works in the market and have taken them out of the country.'

'I have sold nothing for nearly ten years,' I said. 'I live on my savings. If any of my works are for sale then they are being offered by their owners, the people I worked for many years ago. Not me. Not guilty. I'm too old and lazy to be interested in trade.'

The Minister was convinced. Nothing about me or my house suggested wealth or dishonesty.

'Well,' he said. 'It has to stop. It is illegal. The country's resources are being illegally exported under our noses. We are being exploited. You too are being exploited. Collectors in New York are growing rich while your own people are scratching for termites. So . . . it has to stop.'

I shrugged. I had nothing to say. Export control was his affair.

'Tell your friends in the market place,' he said, 'that the next one caught selling your work to a foreigner will be in contravention of our trade and export laws. We'll have to find a place for them in the penal village. Anyone who has works of art to sell must sell them to the government. It is a matter of principle.'

He stood up sharply and towered above me as I reclined beneath the sheet and lizard. 'A travelling exhibition is to be arranged of your work. And an auction sale is to take place . . .'

He sat at the end of my bed and mentioned Paris and Vienna and Toronto and Sydney and, of course, Chicago. He looked pleased on my behalf. 'Naturally, this is a partnership,' he explained. 'You gain, we gain. We gain foreign currency from the sale of your work. Your government will have some . . . discreet money. We will pay it into a safe bank account. In Europe. In Switzerland. That's by far the best. So, you see, if there is an emergency – some medicines are required, for example – then we have the money to buy them. Everybody gains. For you, there is security in your old age. A government house.' I shook my head. 'A car, then, whenever you need it, with a driver. Good food. Comfortable clothes. Fame. We will provide it all.'

'I like good food,' I said. 'I like comfortable clothes. A driver and a car would be most useful. Don't imagine that I am ungrateful or unpatriotic. But there is nothing to exhibit. All my work has gone. It has either been burned with the dead or eaten by parchment lice or shipped off to America by export racketeers. There are a few ornamental gate-plates outside embassies and that is all.'

'What we want,' insisted the Minister, with the single-mindedness of a deaf man, 'are canvases decorated in Siddilic script. Ornamental pieces, works of art, not shop signs and the like.'

'But there are none.'

'Make some. You are a craftsman. It should be simple.'

'If it were that simple,' I said, 'then you would not need to come to me. You could buy what you wanted at every booth in the market. It would be like shopping for potatoes.'

'Well, make an effort then. Meet the grand challenge.'

'I've outgrown challenges.'

'Try,' said the Minister's head of protocol.

*

On Friday I visited my uncles' village in some comfort. I now have a ministerial car at my disposal. And a driver. We swept across the scrub at the end of the Italian road and bumped on the saloon's hydraulic suspension over the last few kilometres to the village. Never before had I been so cool. It is cold at night, of course, in the house. But here in the car I was cool and dry in sunlight. Outside, the sun blistered the paintwork. Goats were too parched to lift their bodies and scurry away.

'Air-conditioning,' said the driver. He peeked in his mirror to enjoy my response. I nodded. I looked impressed.

'Electric windows,' he added. The windows on either side of me hummed down like melting sheets of ice and the daytime heat curled into the car.

'Stereo cassette,' he said and pushed more buttons. A woman sang to me in English. 'Electric windscreen wipers.' A soapy spurt of liquid ejaculated from under the car bonnet on to the windscreen, turned the dust there into mud, and was whisked away by the silent twin-armed wipers. I am an old man and my problems are multiplying. I had never been so hot and cold, so cosseted and so bothered.

'Reclining seats,' said the driver, 'for siesta.' The leather cushions beneath me began to hum and tip. My legs were lifting, my back was falling, all at government expense.

*

The people at my uncles' village were not impressed. All they wanted was tobacco. The driver handed out a packet of cigarettes. But nobody wanted a light from the car's automatic cigar-lighter. Nobody wanted to smoke. They wanted to hoard their fortune. The driver gave out ice cubes from the icebox in the car. Children held them and watched them slowly disappear, like fool's gold. Nobody remembered my uncles, though our family name was familiar. They pointed me towards the trees. They were superstitious enough to respect the acacia of old men. They waited patiently for the firewood.

*

I come once a year – once a year only – to pay my respects at the acacia in the village of my uncles. I come after my birthday and tie a twist of white linen to a branch, a strip of cloth every year.

The tree was now a ragamuffin of flapping tatters, from white to grey to nearly black. There was more linen than leaf. In the old days I came by donkey and then later by bus and now by air-conditioned limousine. In the distance, beyond the walls of the acacia wood, I could hear the stereo cassette of my driver and the shrieks of the children. A touch of reality amongst the reveries.

I took the fresh, newly laundered strip of linen from my pouch and carefully wound it twice round the one living branch. I tied it with a firm knot and stepped back with the delicate care of an egret. Slowly – and not without some pain – I urinated into the earth at the roots of my tree. I had

carried out both the written and the private rituals. Then I
sat and prayed. I prayed – even at this late dry stage in my
rigidly geometric life – for Lily Death.

This is what we were taught as children, that when God
created Death he created two sorts, Lily Death and Moon
Death. The choice is ours, depending on the way we live
our lives. The lily is gregarious. It thrives amongst its own
kind. It sends out shoots which replace and survive it after
death. The moon is solitary and childless. It has no
offshoots. But when it dies, it rises to live again. I had lived
a moon life. Was I to die and rise again? Was the reward of
solitude on earth immortality of some kind?

These days, of course, the choice is not the same. They
have cleared the lilies from the river. The moonshine is
damped out by street lights and car lamps. Nowadays, one
selects either cremation or interment. It's ashes or bones.
We choose the nature of our death by the way we live our
lives. Accusations are made against cigarettes and alcohol,
animal fats and partners in bed.

So back to the limousine and a cool drive to the city,
praying in the stench of button cloth and recycled air for
deliverance from Moon Death. So back across scrub to my
Evening Desk in the inner room.

*

Starting a piece of work is a simple matter for those with
purpose: a desk, some fine inks and brushes, a little chalk
dust (blotting paper is untrustworthy) and a good light are
all that are required.

Exercises first. The calligrapher's hands are tense from mixing his inks, perhaps, or from oversleeping with bad dreams. They must be relaxed. The nervousness must be worked out on scrap paper until the pen and brush strokes are unhesitant, firm and decisive. Then he can embark on the warp and weft of design, on the complex challenges of reconciling the age-old rules which govern the placing of diacritical signs with the vexatious oddities of Siddilic orthography. And now the letters must be worked again to develop fully the equilibrium of dimensions, to reveal balance and rhythm, to express meaning through form. Then the calligrapher should leave his work and eat a little, walk perhaps to a friend's house, bathe, sleep a little. Let the letters brew. He is seeking beauty of the highest intellectual order, the most contemplative, the most civilised and sophisticated. There can be no haste.

Then, refreshed, the calligrapher looks at his first drafts again. He studies them at another desk, under a new light. The decorative themes curl around the letters under his gaze. The kufic and cursive debate before his eyes and present their conclusions. He sits with clean parchment, newly mixed inks, his head not spinning but calm with certainties. This is the easiest and the final draft.

*

I have not been so fortunate. The Minister's head of protocol came today, chewing gum. He inquired about the progress of my great work. Exhibition dates, he said, had been arranged.

'Well,' I explained, 'I have nothing to show you.'

'Then start quickly. You don't have time.'

'I am an old man,' I said. 'I have lost my talents.' I held up a (frankly) excessively shaky hand. 'I've sat at my three desks for two weeks. I have wasted a ream of paper and a half-kilo of ink. Nothing comes. I don't have ideas any longer. You'd better cancel your exhibitions.'

The aide-de-camp looked severely discountenanced. He rolled his chewing gum round his mouth. He looked around the house for some evidence of deceit.

'The Minister isn't going to be pleased,' he said eventually. 'We had an agreement with you.'

I shrugged. I hadn't agreed to anything.

'You've been using the government car! You've been using the government driver! Corruption! Fraud!'

I shrugged again. My hand was really shaking.

'You'll die in prison,' he said. 'We'll burn your house.' He extemporised dreadful fates for a few moments. Then he put up his hands, palms out, at chest level, to indicate that he had discovered a solution and that the threats were now ended. 'Say nothing to the Minister,' he said. 'The Minister has made it my responsibility. You understand. I can make it easy for you. You won't let me down because I can be a very cruel man. Call your servant.'

Sabino came through from the yard and sat down, as instructed, on the tiled floor. The aide-de-camp lit a cigarette and drew on it a few times until its ash burned bright. Then he stubbed it out on Sabino's head. The odour of burnt hair joined the smell of tobacco. Sabino did not seem to feel anything except fear and apprehension.

105

The aide-de-camp and head of Ministerial protocol took the gum from his mouth and ground it, too, into Sabino's scalp. 'There,' he said.

'Bravo.'

'This is just to give you an idea,' he explained. 'Now, to business.' He placed a thick envelope of bank notes on Sabino's head. It balanced there. A fortune. 'That should help you find inspiration,' he said, and left my house with only a fraction of the ceremony with which he had entered it. I have seen many strange things in my life and met many foolish men – but this was the strangest and he was the most foolish.

*

I was spending more and more time on my bed in the company of my gecko. I could think of little but work. But I produced nothing at my desks except doodles in geometric arabesque, mockeries of script. I slept on my back as recommended by the great calligrapher, Mir Ali of Tabriz. He had been thus inspired to devise Nasta'liq, the hanging script of the Muslims. A partridge had appeared to him in a dream and instructed him to shape letters like the wings of a bird. But all I dreamt of was young, young girls. Should I shape letters like young girls for the Minister's great exhibition?

*

Sabino has fled from me. He fears for his life. Now I have

no one to prepare my food, to wash my gowns, to walk into the market for my few provisions.

I walk each day at dusk, just as the moon starts to show itself low on the horizon, to what remain of the market booths. I enjoy myself. People call out to me as they used to when I had a booth of my own. I am a celebrity here, now that the Minister has visited me and Americans have made off with my shop fronts. I buy some fish and a few vegetables. I sit in the Syrian's bar and drink tea while small boys, on hire for a few coins, run to fetch my clean washing or to purchase some heavy item. The Syrian sits with me and complains bitterly: custom is bad, too many laws, too many taxes, the young are disrespectful, an honest man cannot make his honest fortune, thieves everywhere, nobody knows how hard he works, life is cruel and expensive, the heat.

'Tell me, sir,' he asked me one day. 'What must a businessman do? He must follow the market, am I correct? Supply and demand. You are involved in this, so you will understand . . .' He paused to order fresh tea and to whet my curiosity. 'When that first American bought Duni's shop front, my ears were prickling like any good businessman's. Three thousand dollars! For a shop front? Well, I saw a chance. The market was full of tourists. My bar was full of tourists. All they talked of was you, your work, Siddilic script. I sat with them at these tables, to improve my English. Did I know you, they wanted to know. Did you have any work for sale? Not shop fronts. Shop fronts were too big. Something small. Something that could be rolled up and taken home in a suitcase. Well, no, I had nothing. But a businessman never says no. "Come back in three days," I told them, "and then, maybe, I will have found something. But it will be expensive, of course." "Never mind 'expensive'," they said. So . . .' The Syrian smiled at his own cunning. 'I went to somebody – let us not say who – and told him: "I can pay such and such for good Siddilic script. By the master, of course. Nothing too large, mind. With the master's authentic signature, naturally!" And in two days my friend returned with a parchment. A very nice piece. A good clear signature.

'I wasn't fooled. The design was beautiful but the ink had been applied by an amateur in a hurry. The ink was poor school ink and had dried unevenly. It was a copy. But a skilfully signed copy. I paid my friend such and such. And one day later I sold to an American for such and such and such. Good business. Perfectly legal. What am I, an expert on scripts? How should I know?

'So, I told my friend: "Good, quite good, bring me some more, but sell only to me." This is also good business practice: control the supply, establish a modest monopoly, wait for the price to rise, sell. Simple. Second nature to a Syrian. Imagine, then, my store room full of your beautiful work, rising in price day by day, minute by minute. I was going to be a rich, rich man. Already my friend was a wealthy man from the money I had paid him. Already I was dreaming of dying in Damascus, of seeing my brothers in Aleppo for the first time in twenty years, of sitting with my toes in the Euphrates, of waving goodbye to business forever.

'Then what occurs at the airport? They arrest my

American. They seize his parchment. They let him fester at the police barracks for a few days while they threaten him with evading their new export regulations. Control of Antiquities and Artefacts (Backdated). They insult his wife. They frighten his children. The American ambassador makes visits to the Minister. An aid deal is agreed on. The American is released and sent back to his big house in Massachusetts. The Minister's man visits me. "Never again," he tells me, "sell a work of art to a foreigner. If you do, you're in big trouble. You're in big trouble anyway. Tread lightly." Maybe my trading licence won't get renewed. Maybe my passport will be required for scrutiny at the Minister's office. Now I'll never die in Damascus. Why? All because I am a businessman. Supply and demand.'

We went, two old men with waning dreams, to the storeroom behind the bar. There, beside the crates of cola and fruit drinks, the bottles of wine and beer, was a canvas case full of parchments. Indecipherability was the keynote to these forgeries, with every stroke over-ornate and uneven. Misplaced accents hovered uncertainly over misspelt words. All were signed with my name.

\*

Finally I dreamt my dream of inspiration. I dreamt of a large gallery full of smart Europeans in their best clothes, walking slowly round the exhibits with expensive catalogues. I stood in a European suit, a young man once again, pointing out some fine detail to a beautiful woman.

'Here,' I was saying, 'I have misplaced the vowel sound so that this word reads "Moon" instead of "Man". And here are letters which do not exist in Siddilic and which no one can decipher. And there I have pressed so hard on my pen that the nib has snapped. So that sign there is not an accent but a blot.' The woman smiled appreciatively. The gallery applauded. Rich men shook my hand. The Minister shook my hand. I saw the Syrian rinsing his toes in a wide river. I saw Sabino in my courtyard. I saw my acacia throwing out new shoots.

When I woke, the envelope of bank notes was lying unopened at the side of my bed. I dressed and hurried to the Syrian's bar.

'Your story moved me,' I told him. 'It was my fault that you lost your money. I carry the guilt.'

'Well, maybe,' said the Syrian.

'Here, take this envelope. Give me the scrolls.'

The Syrian saw the thickness of the envelope and did not haggle. He promised me free tea at his bar 'until the angels take you up to Paradise in recognition of your kindness and your honesty'. He put the envelope into his safe and hung the key on a gold chain at his throat. He put his finger to his lips. 'Say nothing,' he told me. 'This is between friends.'

*

Now the Minister has his exhibits and I am working to contribute just one genuine piece of my own. My last work of calligraphy, the work which was intended to be sealed in a tube of bamboo and burned at my funeral, is now to go instead to Vienna and Paris and Chicago. It is my Sins and Virtues.

I sit at my desks, intimate and scholarly, plaiting knots of kufic script, the stems foliated, the heads floriated. I curve patterns of letters, leaves and tendrils. Tightly disciplined parades of verticle strokes march across the parchment to come to attention at undergrowth concealing fabulous animals. Blooms and blossoms fall amongst keywords in plain geometric patterns.

I have divided the paper into four squares and there in each square is a virtue embracing a vice. I plead guilty to Lust, but I name Virginity in mitigation. I admit to Selfishness but call upon Self-Awareness in my defence. I decorate with half-palmettes the verticles of Misanthropy and list the names of those I failed to help. But I claim, too, the virtue of Tolerance and display an empty nameless list of those I ever intentionally harmed. My greatest virtue has been the virtue of Talent. I inscribe it large and plain. Simplicity is the mark of the craftsman. Talent shares its box with Deceit, the same word in Siddilic for Forgery. 'ALL THIS WORK IS FALSE,' I have written and decorated in gold. Now my Sins and Virtues are complete. I leave the manuscript unsigned . . .

*

The Minister's man tried to persuade me to follow my exhibition to all the galleries in the world, to give talks and interviews, to be present at the great auction. But I explained that I was too frail for travel and the aide-de-camp was not insistent.

The Minister is very pleased. He came to compliment me on my exertion and to repeat his promise of luxuries in my old age. He inquired about the possibility of more works. But I explained to him Supply and Demand. Flood the market, I told him, and the price goes down.

'You are famous worldwide,' he said, sitting at the end of my bed, watching the gecko in the folds of my bed sheet. 'Our country is now highly regarded. Art is important in Europe and America.'

He rose to leave. 'One small point,' he said. 'There is one parchment which is unsigned . . .'

'Does it matter?'

'For the price, the value, that's all. Art buyers like to know that they are buying the genuine article. If there is no signature . . .'

'Sell that one cheaply, then,' I suggested. 'That is good practice in business, too, to have something cheap amongst the more expensive.'

'Excellent,' said the Minister. 'You are more worldly than I had imagined.'

\*

I have left instructions with the Syrian and with Duni, the ironmonger, and all those that know me in the market, that when I die they should burn my body and take my ashes in a vase to the village of my uncles. There they should bury me beneath the acacia. Duni asked me about my Sins and

Virtues, but I explained that I had lived such a solitary life that I had none.

'What, not even a little minor failing once in a while?' he asked.

'No, nothing,' I said. 'My conscience is clean.' The sinlister, I reminded him, must be free from sin. It is the custom and the regulation.

*

I pass between my various desks with very little purpose now. Occasionally I take out ink and paper, just for old times' sake, and doodle for a while. But I am not interested in letters. The quest for Meaning in Form belongs to an age long past. I often draw a forest of trees, almost bare and leafless, with the moon hovering on the horizon. Is it dawn or dusk? Soon we all shall know.

*Six*

# Electricity

'Neglect,' says Awni, the Rest House warden. 'For one hundred years we have been neglected. Now we are remembered!' And who claims credit? Warden Awni does. 'My petitions worked the trick,' he says. He displays carbon copies. Anyone is welcome to read his fawning paragraphs, to Ministers and Civil Servants. Now the town supplicant has turned braggart. 'You will be pleased to learn that electrical power is to be installed in your town during the Dry,' informs the framed ministerial letter which Awni has tacked to the veranda wall. The

Rest House is amongst the first dozen buildings to be equipped with sockets and fittings.

We know better. Awni's petitions are not the cause: they are too frequent and too disperse. He petitions for a road surface, for a petrol licence, for a landing strip, for the removal of the schoolteacher ('Honoured Minister, we have amongst us one who, like a kittle beetle, disseminates anxiety . . .'). He petitions for a transfer elsewhere, to the town or the coast or the salt lake resorts. He is ignored. No, it is the Minister's personal secretary who deserves our gratitude. His neighbour is landowner Nepruolo. They own adjacent houses in the city's New Extension. They have vacation cottages on the Mu coast. Their wives are stalwarts of the same club; their children bicker at the same school.

We can construct their conversation: Nepruolo calls upon his neighbour to present a basket of fresh candy gourds 'grown on my land in the Flat Centre'. Our land. 'They would be larger and sweeter,' he says, as the Secretary's children sever the fruit from the creeper and slice the crisp white flesh. 'But . . . well, do not let me bore you with farming talk. Without good water pumps during the Dry, the gourds take siesta. Electric pumps are best, but we do not have electricity, so . . . small fruit.' The Secretary squeezes a lime over his crescent of fruit and commiserates: '*I* should not want land there without electricity . . . but if there were electricity then the thought of a small gourd farm with a comfortable lodge is attractive.' 'Land I can provide cheaply to a friend and neighbour,' says Nepruolo. 'Electricity I cannot.' The

Secretary enjoys his fruit. Soon he will have larger, sweeter candy gourds of his own. He will add another document to the Minister's endorsement file, with a pencilled cross for his signature. He will stamp the document 'PP1' (top Project Priority) and then he will talk terms with Nepruolo.

All that Awni can construct is his letter of thanks. Copies are tacked to the veranda wall. 'Honoured Minister and Friend, We thank you for the gift of Progress through Electrical Power . . .'

\*

Good to its word, the government has erected pylons. It has laid cables. It has wired the hospital, the school, government buildings, Nepruolo land. In a few weeks we will have electricity. The Rest House is to be hung with glass lanterns in lemon and green and orange. 'They will be mangoes of light,' says Awni. 'Mangoes of light all along the veranda.' Electricity becomes familiar to us, domesticated as shining mangoes.

More strange are the electricians, clean workers with hard fingers, who have come from the city in neat trucks and taken up noisy residence in Awni's best rooms. Hear these men sing and argue as they work! They bury flayed mechanical limbs of wire deep into wall plaster. They handle the tendons and sinews, the long red arteries, the blue veins, with the intimacy of surgeons. The children stand close to dive and wrestle for snips of wire and plastic which fall to the ground. How will it be, they ask, when the Minister and the President of the Company arrive to switch on the current? Will the electricity flow like water, first lighting dull lamps and spinning slow fans close to the generator, then running through those thin and shiny filaments to the police station, the school, along the Rest House veranda – mango by mango – until it reaches the hospital to drip and spurt, like a farmer's furthest tap, amongst the sick-beds? Not like water, explain the electricians. 'But strong and all at once.'

The children do not understand. How can electricity be instantaneous, no sooner in the town centre than on its fringes? How can it be so heedlessly rapid when it has been so slow, when it has taken so many years to reach us here at all?

'Which is nearest to your brain, your nose or your arse?' tease the electricians. Children slap their noses. 'But which can you twitch first? Let's race. Boys, be noses; girls, be bums. And when we say *Now* send a message from your brain, to twitch and shake. Who will win?' Boys and girls – and old men, too – twitch and shake. The noses cannot beat the bums. 'So now you understand,' say the electricians. 'It takes exactly as long for a message to travel from here to here' (an electrician's fingers span the prettiest girl's face from forehead to nose) 'as it does from here to here!' (Now he stoops and stretches, touching her buttocks and head.) 'Electricity is like that. Like a message from the brain, no sooner sent than received.' The President of the Company presses a lever and every light on the veranda will shine. The hospital will be bright as soon as the police station. The fan in the schoolhouse will turn no sooner than the wheel of the water pump on Nepruolo land. At home that night, by candlelight, mothers and fathers gravely twitch and shake for their educated children.

*

'Beware of electricity,' says the schoolteacher. 'You will become addicts.' His comments are directed at Awni who has been polishing his mangoes and listing the electrical equipment which he has ordered (cheaply and furtively) from the electricians: a modern ice-box, table lamps, a liquidiser for expensive drinks. 'Kittle beetle,' he says, but the teacher persists. He has lived in the city; he has travelled abroad and trained in Denmark. He is playful in the European manner, joking but not laughing. He alone in the town has lived with science and light. 'Beware, beware.'

What must it be like to have sharp, strong light at hand, on the flick of a finger? To have cool fresh air fanning the Dry mid-days? To have ice in every drink? To be visited, like other towns, by the cinema truck? 'Addictive,' repeats the teacher. He recalls for us a day in Denmark. 'I was reading in the conservatory,' he says. 'I was alone in the house. Jens was teaching. Lotte was teaching. Their children, Christoffer and Kirsten, were at school. I was being economical at the request of the Minister of Power who complained daily in the newspapers and on the television that Danes had become reckless with electricity. All that comforted me was fire, a radio and a reading

121

lamp.' He shows how the appliances were ranged around him, how leads led to plugs, how plugs fitted tightly into sockets on the Jorgensen walls. He demonstrates with a saucer how the energy disc on the electric meter was spinning as gently as a seed mast, its calibrations individually distinct. The saucer turns precariously on the teacher's finger.

'There was nothing I could do,' he says, 'to stop that disc from spinning; eating power, eating money.' If he disconnected the lamp and fire and radio still the flat, metal monitor crept anti-clockwise, notching up amperes on the digital display. Elsewhere in the Jorgensen home gadgets slumbered, drip-fed by electricity: the fridge, the fish-tank, the door-bell, the telephone-answering machine, the yoghurt-maker, the deep-freeze in the garage, the kitchen clock, the water-heater. (With the naming of each item we beg for explanations.) 'But if I could not stop it,' he says, 'then I could make it go fast. One flick at the side of the electric fire with my toe. More heat! And the energy disc begins to trot. What fun we would have when the children came home. Christoffer, Kirsten and I had devised an experiment.'

At last the twins returned from school. Christoffer was apprehensive. (What if his parents arrived mid-escapade?) Kirsten was over-excited and impatient. She wished to begin immediately, haphazardly. 'But I insisted on scientific strategy and order,' says the schoolmaster. 'We started in our own rooms and worked outwards and downwards to the spinning disc in the conservatory. Everything electric, from the lights to typewriters, we set in motion.' He traces a quickening circle in the air with a chalky finger. He grins at the memory. The energy disc was gaining speed. Bedside lamps, electric blankets, convector heaters, a tape-recorder, a train set, a sewing machine. The downstairs rooms were the most prized. Kirsten was the first to lay claim to the clamorous appliances in the toilet and the laundry room. The washing-machine embarked upon its longest, most war-like cycle. The tumble-dryer barrelled a tornado of hot air. The water-heater catered silently for pipes. Towel-rails and steam-irons shared overloaded sockets with sun-lamps and electric toothbrushes. Kirsten was too small to reach the toiletry cabinet. The schoolteacher was sum-moned. He opened it and handed down her father's shaver and her mother's hair-dryer. They dangle-danced from their high socket on springing cords, bouncing, blowing and chewing at the bathroom rug.

Christoffer was busy in the Jorgensen living-room. 'Table lamp, standard lamp, fire, television,' he yelled, patiently turning silence into buzz and buzz into roar. 'Stereo, video, radio.' And then, to the shudder of a rudimentary, over-amplified chord, 'Guitar!'

Now they hurried to reach the kitchen: cooker, toaster, mixer, grinder, blender, carver, polisher, sweeper, dish-washer, kettle. Another radio, another fire, another small television set. Fountain. Fairy lights. At last, they were done. Together, they dispatched the garden mower down the lawn. At the extent of its lead, it tugged and growled at the free, long grass beyond its reach, like a tethered, liverish goat. The house and garden were a powered cauldron of heat and light and sound.

How did the spinning disc survive this onslaught? The teacher lowers his voice and leans forward to tell. 'It had disappeared,' he says. 'It was moving so fast that we could no longer see it. I climbed on a chair and tried to view it from above. But no, nothing. Only the faint smell of scorched metal and a cloudy smoking of the glass.' This is the point – with the teacher high on the chair, the twins holding their ears and laughing, the Jorgensen home clamouring like a nightmare – where Jens and Lotte returned. 'We screamed our explanations. We retraced our routes and unplugged. We picked the fibres from the shaver; we unpicked the keys of typewriters; we replaced the scorched towelling on the ironing board; we rewired the lawn-mower; we patched up the burns on Lotte's hand (she had leaned on the toaster); we apologised to neighbours; we blushed. But, now, here is a mystery. Once the house had cooled and quietened, still the energy disc was missing. The Jorgensens said it must have disintegrated at speed, like a meteorite, and its flaming pieces had fallen into the workings of the meter. Certainly the digits on the ampage counter never budged again. But I can't accept so prosaic an explanation.'

We look to the teacher for *his* explanation. But he is being playful. He has none. He is teasing us, that is all. 'Soon,' he says, 'thanks to Awni's obsequious petitions, this town, with its oil lamps, its hand pumps, its long nights, its stillness, will be a powered cauldron of heat and light and sound. It will spin with electricity. And it will disappear.'

\*

Awni has closed the solemn inner room of the Rest House restaurant to all but electricians. He will give no explanation. Guests, travellers, and those townspeople with time and money, now eat and drink at crowded tables on the veranda. It is marvellously successful: stranger jostles with stranger; titbits are exchanged; trays of food are passed from hand to hand to inaccessible tables; whispers are inaudible, everybody shouts.

'Be patient,' Awni tells his customers. 'Soon these inconveniences will be forgotten and my rooms reopened . . .' But those on the veranda are not listening. A bat-moth is flapping wildly amongst the tables and customers are trying to read its signs. It pauses for an instant of rest on a plate of pomatoes and is caught. An upturned glass jug – hastily emptied of water over veranda floor and customer shoes – is lowered over the moth's arched black wings. The eaters and drinkers gather round and wait. For a minute or so, the moth strikes the jug with its wings, and quivers – but then it quietens, spreads itself across the fruit, and plays dead. Now the customers are as equally still and silent. All eyes trace a line along the bat-moth's body and down its red-tipped tail spike. The spike is pointing at the policeman's wife. The moth is telling her fortune. She counts the grey smudges along the moth's still back: seven children! She measures its wing-latch: long life! She peers closely and nervously at the four black wings: the love wing, the money wing, the pleasure wing are perfect. But one hind wing is ragged at the edge, an injury. 'Bad health,' says the policeman's wife. She lifts the glass jug and the bat-moth flaps and spirals once again amongst the tables.

'Soon these inconveniences will be forgotten,' repeats Awni, striking at the moth with his hand. But still his customers are not listening. Now the policeman's wife is standing with her back against the shuttered window of the restaurant (her face lit like an actress by the bending flames of candle and lamps) and is singing.

> The night is warm,
> The night is long;
> We are alone, alone, alone.

There are tears in the electricians' eyes as they stand at their table on the veranda and raise their glasses to the singer. These are the times that their grandfathers spoke of: music, food and good humour. 'Soon,' says Awni, 'there will be improvements.'

*

In daylight, the veranda becomes a workplace. The electricians rest their reels of wire against chairs and spread their drills and screws and fittings on tables. They are working on the electrification of the inner room and on its preparation for the opening ceremony. Warden Awni has tacked a notice (hand-decorated and lettered by a calligrapher in the city) on the veranda wall: 'The Warden of this Rest House, in pursuance of his Honoured Duties towards Residents and Travellers, announces that, to mark the Advent of Electrical Power, Modernisations are in process with all the Urgency required to secure their completion in time for the Visit to these Premises of our Friend and Benefactor, the Minister, and Representatives . . .'

Who can read any further without first resting, drawing breath and sneaking forward to explore within? None of the townspeople, certainly. Curiosity impels them along the veranda to the open door, through which electricians are passing with the fussing preoccupation of weevils in cake. There, just as Awni has promised, is the box of glass mangoes, dull and disappointing. A wooden crate, the size of four coffins, contains what the children have identified as a small white truck. It is the new ice-box. Cartons of cola and beer and fruit drinks await refrigeration. Table lamps with New York Skylines as a friezed motif are packed in shredded bark. A liquidiser gleams beside its newly fitted socket. And against the far wall is a square, flat box, as wide as a demon's cartwheel. 'This is my centrepiece,' says Awni, but will say no more. 'It is the world's largest petition,' suggests the teacher. 'Awni is respectfully requesting the provision of a wetter climate. Next time it rains Awni will take the credit.' But the children know better. They have climbed on tables and peered into the open top of the box. Inside are a set of aeroplane propellers, cut from the heaviest, the most polished and tiger-grained tarbony, each blade the height of a man.

There are no secrets in this town ('At least, none that we

know of'). So when Awni banishes all the children from the veranda and herds them at the rim of the Rest House land with the youngest and cruellest of the electricians to stand guard, we all leave our homes and our fields to join the crowd and call out, 'What's the fuss? What are we missing?' 'Keep back,' says Awni. 'You'll find out in good time.' 'Find out what? Won't you tell?'

Awni closes the door from the veranda to the restaurant. All we can hear now is the hammering and chipping and nailing of electricians at work. He stands with his back to the door facing out over the veranda towards the crowd. The youngest and the cruellest electrician can control children with stern words but he cannot hold the crowd. It edges forward until it lines the veranda steps.

'What's the fuss, Awni?'

'There is no fuss. *You're* making the fuss. Go home!'

'What's going on?'

'Nothing . . . improvements . . .'

'What improvements? Why can't the children see? What are they making for you in there? An electric woman?'

Even Awni laughs at this.

'Listen,' he says, coming close to us. 'Be patient. You see these?' He points to the petitions and lofty announcements which decorate the wall. 'Now this town is on the map. We have electricity. Soon the road will be made up. Then we will have an airstrip, a cinema, a radio transmitter, a factory, our own abattoir. But first we have electricity . . . so let us be ambitious, let us have the best electricity in the world. Let the Minister come here and see how we excel with electricity. Then he will nod and say to

128

himself, "Ah, that town has vision. Send engineers, send aeronauts, send projectionists, send radio operators, send industrialists, send slaughtermen. Send money. Turn that town into a city!" '

'But what are you hiding, Warden Awni?'

'I *will* show you,' he says. We crowd behind him as he throws back the door to the inner room of the restaurant. Inside, the electricians are standing on chairs and tables, their arms lifting and pushing towards the ceiling.

'Let us see. What is it? What is it?'

A thin girl crawls past Awni into the room and walks into the centre of the circle of electricians. She looks up and then returns to the crowd at the door.

'They're fixing the propeller to the ceiling,' she says. 'They're making an aeroplane.'

Awni stands aside for us all to enter and admire. 'It is my gift to this town,' he says, 'to mark the visit of the Minister and the installation of electrical power. It is the largest, the finest fan in the land.'

The last screw of the fitting which attaches Awni's fan to the ceiling is tightened. An electrician pushes against one of the huge polished blades. It turns resentfully, unpowered, its tip nearly reaching the restaurant walls. Its shadow, cast by the light from the veranda windows, is a huge black moth. 'Solid wood, solid metal,' says Awni boastfully. 'A monumental fan.'

*

The first to arrive is the Minister's Secretary. His black

Peugeot has been dusted grey by the journey over bad, dry roads. He has seen maned deer, quibbling flocks of ground-thrush, a mesmerised bandicoot caught mid-carriageway by the engine roar. He sees gnawed gourds and damaged saplings – the work of Baird tapirs and their comic snouts. All good pot animals, and sitting targets, too. The thought of land here becomes more attractive. The comfortable family lodge with a small gourd farm transforms into a hotel for hunters, weekend marksmen keen on game but untempted by treks and danger and patience. Is there profit here, good business? When he first sees the Rest House he becomes more certain. This is no competition for his hotel: it is a timid, wind-swept little coop in wood and plaster, badly situated and poorly equipped. What idiot arranged for the Minister to switch on the current from there? Tin-pot town. Tin-pot people.

The Minister's Secretary waits in his car a field's distance from the Rest House. Soon the army jeeps will arrive with the soldiers and ceremonial equipment. The Secretary is free to scheme. Later that day he will investigate Nepruolo land and select a good site, close to the road and the police station, but wind and neighbour free. Electricity has come; the gourds will fatten. Nepruolo will be kept to his promise. Landowner and Secretary, as ever, will see eye-to-eye – particularly as they now share interests in the same town. A newly surfaced road – now, that would benefit both. Remove those potholes. Lay that dust with tarmac. Weekending hunts-men, purses full and game bags empty, speed to the country: they pass brimming convoys of Nepruolo trucks delivering plump-as-dove candy gourds to city whole-salers. The Secretary can see it all. He will speak dreams to his colleagues, the secretaries of appropriate ministries.

Once the jeeps and the black car draw up outside the Rest House the crowd begins to gather. They will wait all day for the Minister to arrive. They babble and laugh and miss nothing. The Minister's Secretary is perplexed. He turns to the commander of the six soldiers for explanations. 'What are they doing?' he asks.

'They're shaking their backsides and snitching their noses.'

'And who is this?' Awni has come out on to his veranda and begun an oration.

'Honoured Minister and friend,' he says. 'We welcome you . . .'

'Not yet. Save your prostrations. I am not the Minister. I am his Secretary.'

Awni beams and clasps the visitor by the elbow. 'Then we have corresponded,' he says, and points to his gallery of documents. 'I am Warden Awni. Here is my petition for electricity, you remember? And here, today, is the outcome.' He raises his arms in self-congratulation and swings the newly hung glass lanterns in yellow, green and orange. 'But I cannot claim all the credit. The Minister, too, deserves our thanks . . .'

The Minister's Secretary begins to wonder whether he is the victim of some subtle irony. 'These people?' He indicates those few in the crowd who are still racing bums and noses. 'What is the point which they are making? Who are they?'

'Townspeople, Secretary. They have come to admire the electricity and the Minister.'

'Yes, but what is this shaking?'

'Ah,' says Awni, happy to provide the simple explanation. 'They are sending messages from their brains. No sooner sent than received. Like electrical power!'

Now the Secretary is convinced that his hotel will have no competition. The Warden of the Rest House is as mad as a mongoose. Perhaps it would be politic – just for the day – to lock him out of sight. The Minister is a man not keen on aberrations. But the Warden has hurried off, busy with preparations and self-esteem. The Minister's Secretary is left to deploy his soldiers ('Subdue those shakers. Let no one pass') and then spy out his land. Soon the ceremonial will be over and business can begin.

*

The Minister has arrived in a motorcade of limousines, windscreen-wipers rinsing the dust. This town has never known so eminent, so punctilious an assembly. But why so quiet? All that the townspeople can hear – they are roped off and distant – is the commotion of Awni's servilities. He introduces his guests: he indicates his fan, his table lamps, his ice-box, the coloured veranda lights, bright with polish. He applauds his foresight and planning: there is the liquidiser already filled with unmixed cocktail, its sweet gourd, mint-water, cheap Korean whisky, salt and sayoot powder, impatient for a powered whisk.

But except for Awni the inner room is stiffly silent. The guests are tightly packed. They cannot circulate and chatter. They do not like to jostle and shout to friends with the Minister so near. What can electricians say, in whispers, when pressed so close and warmly to the President of their company? How can the policeman's wife amuse the unsmiling pressmen and photographers when she cannot stretch her arms and sing? How intimately, how cunningly, should land-owner Nepruolo address the Minister's Secretary now that they are wedged shoulder to shoulder: as a neighbour, colleague, friend, partner, collaborator? As a stranger? Schoolteacher, policeman, barrack captain, town doctor, bullock-gelder, merchant's wife – all are close tongued.

'Let us get on,' the Minister commands an aide. The Minister is not impressed by fans and liquidisers. What he loves most is the privacy of his limousine.

It is now night. The townspeople stand, roped off in moonlight. The last wild flames are snuffed on candles and oil lamps in the Rest House. The Minister makes a brief speech. He has had the personal satisfaction, he says, of fighting and winning the political battles for the electrification of forgotten communities in the Flat Centre. It is a project close to his heart. How he wishes that government business was less exacting – then he could act with lizard-impulse and accept Warden Awni's generous offer of a few days' rest amongst the fine people of the town. (Here the Minister discharges a smile for the policeman's wife.) But, no, he must settle for the lesser pleasure of service and duty. He must return shortly to the city. But first . . . 'Let me leave you with a fond memory of your Minister.' He grasps the ceremonial power-switch and pulls.

It is startling how light can shorten distance. The Rest House – now a grid of hard white with a diadem of coloured lamps – has leapt towards the townspeople. Every face at the window of the inner room is distinct. Every word is clear. Even the far fields have closed in, defined by the stipples of illumination at the school, the hospital, the police station, and on Nepruolo land. The town has shrunk. Only the sky and dawn seem more distant.

Awni's guests are a little startled, too, though not by electricity. Most of them have stood before in false light on visits to the city. No, they are startled by Awni's liquidiser which slices into action almost before the lights have penetrated to the corners of the room and thrown shadows over blinking faces. They all turn to stare at the liquidiser, labouring them a cocktail, and there is laughter. Applause, too.

It is a magic charm. Tongues are loosened. Electricians shake their President's hand. Pressmen smile at tradesmen. The merchant's wife – 'not for the first time', it is whispered – offers her cheek to the bullock-gelder. The Minister discharges more smiles for the policeman's wife. Nepruolo and the Minister's Secretary embrace. It is a celebration.

'Now we are remembered!' calls Awni through the open window.

Bald men, and women with naked arms, are the first to notice that the wind is rising. The room shivers. Cigarette smoke speeds back at the smoker. Cocktail glasses rattle. 'There will be rain' or 'The moon is belching' or 'Expect a birth in town tonight', comment the superstitious. The rest button their jackets and send Awni to close the shutters.

*

But the breeze does not abate. Now it buffets the inner walls and hammers a passage between the guests. The squall is growing from within.

'My fan!' says Awni. 'I had forgotten.'

How could he forget his centrepiece, his gift to the town? It has responded slowly to power – its wooden arms too broad and heavy to rotate freely. It has spun like a seed mast, gradually picking up speed, gradually herding and pocketing the air in the Rest House. Now it is in command.

'That *is* a large fan,' says Nepruolo. 'It's as wide as the room . . .' All conversation has stopped and Awni's fan is the centre of attention.

'Minister,' demands Awni. 'Have you ever seen such a fan before, in all your travels, in all the fine buildings you have visited . . .?'

'Never,' says the Minister, thinking of the discreet, silent air-conditioning in his own office, home and car. 'I believe this fan to be unique.'

'I dedicate this unique fan to the Minister,' declaims Awni, 'in thanks for the provision of electrical power . . .'

The guests – their faces chilled and rosy from staring

windward – feel obliged to applaud both Minister and fan.

Still the giant blades are gaining speed. They shovel air from the heights of the room and pitch it at the heads of honoured guests.

'See, see!' cries Awni, blocking all escape through the veranda door. 'Now everyone is cool. Feel how cool we are!'

The fan's shadow, cast darkly across the ceiling by electric light, beats and flaps, reaches and dips, like a flail-dancer, spinning faster and giddier. The fan has out-stripped electricity: it is self-propelled, driven by its own turbulence. Clothes tug tightly on bodies, eyes are lashed with tears, plates and glasses tumble from shelves and shatter, as squall gusts into gale and gale into cyclone. Who there does not fear the electrical storm?

'One place is safe,' says the Minister, putting his arm around the policeman's wife with the intimacy of an uncle. 'At the hub.' They labour against the blast and stand as close as doves in the narrow column of stillness directly beneath the fan.

'It is simple physics,' explains the Minister, relishing the plump songstress in his arms. 'Locate the eye of the storm and escape all turbulence. Here, we are quite safe.'

Their fellow guests recede further from them, flattened and crouching against the Rest House walls. Those who dare watch the ceiling, but they can see no fan. It is moving so fast that it has disappeared. They cup their eyes against the wind and look again. But no, nothing. Only the faint smell of scorched wires, and a cloudy smoking of the air.

The first indication that the storm has peaked is a crack

in the ceiling. The second is a shower of crumbled plaster: half settles lightly on the Minister and his ward, half is pulled into the windy vortex and turned into stinging grapeshot. The third is a sharp detonation. The ceiling can no longer withstand the weight and pressure. It releases Warden Awni's fan. A blade hits the Rest House wall and splinters into a thousand needles of best tarbony. The cyclone is armed.

'Switch off the current,' commands an electrician. (He and his comrades are squashed safely behind the restaurant counter.) But too late. The jagged vanguard of needles reaches the guests. Splinters of tarbony slice flesh and chip wall-plaster; missiles of wood lacerate the New York skylines of table lamps and shatter bulbs; a salvo strikes the ice-box; a single, knotted bolt of timber finishes the cocktail, showering electricians in mint-water, whisky and liquidiser. What remains of the fan kicks and cracks against the ceiling and then, snapping its wiring, falls. The Minister and the policeman's wife – those two doves at the eye of the storm – receive the great weight of the wreckage. One by one, the mangoes on the veranda smoke, burn and fail. Now the only light is the occasional flash of a pressman's camera.

\*

That moonlit veranda . . . what travellers gather there, now that the Rest House has closed and we have the Huntsman Hotel with its garden bar, its pool, its patio restaurant, its cane settees and glass-topped tables? Bats, lizards, goats, ghosts. The children dare not venture too close; their parents, nervous of cracking timber and sagging walls, warn against the truculent spirits of electricity. Awni – turned shopkeeper – petitions for compensation, restitution, revenge.

The schoolteacher is more forgiving. He has time on his hands and his own stool at the Huntsman bar.

'It is a simple matter,' he says, lifting the patch to display the contour of scars across his eye. 'The fan was too large and wilful. It ran too fast.' A saucer turns precariously on the teacher's finger. 'That little Rest House could not take the pressure. The fan disintegrated at speed, like a meteorite.'

Visitors from the city see the logic of this – but the townspeople, avoiding those places where electricity is installed, cannot accept so prosaic an explanation.

# Seven

# The Prospect from the Silver Hill

The company agent – friendless, single, far from home – passed most days alone in a cabin at Ibela-hoy, the Hill Without a Hat. His work was simple. Equipped with a rudimentary knowledge of mineralogy, neat, laborious handwriting, and a skill with ledgers, he had been posted to the high lands to identify the precious metals, the stones, the ores, that (everybody said) were buried there.

This was his life: awake at dawn, awake all day, awake all night. Phrenetic Insomnia was the term. But there were no friends or doctors to make the diagnosis. The agent simply – like a swift, a shark – dared not sleep. He kept moving. He did not close his eyes. At night, at dawn, in the tall heat of the day, he looked out over the land and, watching the shades and colours of the hill and its valley accelerate and reel, he constructed for himself a family and a life less solitary than the one that he was forced to live. He took pills. He drank what little spirit arrived each month with his provisions. He exhausted himself with long, aimless walks amongst the boulders and dry beds. Sometimes he fell forward at work, his nose flattened amongst the gravels on the table, his papers dampened by saliva, his tongue slack. But he did not sleep or close his eyes, though he was still troubled by chimeras, day-dreams, which broke his concentration and (because he was conscious) seemed more substantial and coherent than sleeping dreams. As the men had already remarked amongst themselves when they saw the sacs of tiredness spreading across his upper cheeks and listened to his conversation, the company agent either had a fever or the devil had swapped sawdust for his brain.

Several times a week one of the survey gangs arrived in a company mobile to deposit drill cores of augered rock and sand, pumice and shale, and provide the company agent with a profile of the world twenty metres below his feet. He sorted clays as milky as nutsap and eggstones as worn and weathered as a saint's bead into sample bags. Each rock, each smudge of soil, was condemned. Nothing. Nothing. Nothing. A trace of tin. Nothing.

Once, when he had been at Ibela-hoy for a few weeks only, one of the survey gangs offered to take him down to the lumber station where the woodsmen had established a good still and an understanding with some local women. He sat in the cab of the mobile drilling rig and talked nonstop. That's the loneliest place, he told them, as the mobile descended from the cabin. There aren't even ghosts. He spoke, too, about the wife and children, the companionable life, which he had concocted in his daydreams. How he wished he had a camera at home, he told the men. Then he could have shown them photographs of his family, of his garden in the city, his car, his wedding day.

The men indulged him. He was still a stranger, they reasoned, and starved of company, missing home. He would quieten down once he had a glass in his hand. But they had been wrong. He became louder with every sip. He spoke in a voice which sent the women back into their homes, which sent the men early to bed. The voice said, My sadness is stronger than your drink. Nothing can relieve it. Nothing. A trace of tin. Nothing.

He daydreamed: a lifetime of finding nothing. He dreamed of prospecting the night sky and locating a planet of diamonds or an old, cooled sun of solid gold. But then the company had no need for diamonds or gold. Find us sand, they instructed. Find us brown mud. Send us a palmful of pebbles. He dreamed again, and produced a twist of earth and stone which contained new colours, a seam of creamy nougat in a funnel of tar. His dream delivered the funnel to his company offices. Soon secretaries typed Ibela-hoy for the first time – and a name was coined for the new mineral which he had unearthed. Then his dream transported friends and family to Ibela-hoy. They walked behind him as he set out to map the creamy seam. Together they charted an area the shape of a toadstool. A toadstool of the newest mineral in the world. His daydream provided a telephone and a line of poles. He telephoned the company with the good news. They referred him to the Agency and then to the Ministry. His calls were bounced and routed between switchboards and operators and his story retold a dozen times – but nobody was found with sufficient authority to accept such momentous information or to order his return to home, to sleep.

Send me a dream, he said aloud, in which my wife and my children are brought to the cabin. When I wake, they are there. When I sleep, they are there. We sit at the same table. The two boys tumble on the bed. The baby stands on my thighs with crescent legs and tugs at my nose and hair. My wife and I sit together slicing vegetables at the table. But when he had finished speaking there was no reply from amongst the rocks, no promises. He spoke again, in whispers. Have pity, he said.

Sometimes he wrapped his arms round boulders, warmed by the sun, and embraced them. My wife, he said. He kissed boulders.

Now the men kept their distance. They were polite but no longer generous. There were no more invitations to visit the lumber station – and they became watchful on those occasions when they brought drill cores to the cabin. Does this man know his business, they asked amongst themselves. Can he be trusted to know marl from marble? They waited awkwardly at his door or stood at his window as their plugs of earth were spread and sorted on his bench, the soils washed and sieved, the stones stunned and cracked, the unusual flakes of rocks matched with the specimens in the mineral trays. His fatigue – the second stage – had hardened his concentration. He was engrossed. He lowered his head and smelled the soil. He sucked the roundest pebbles. He rubbed stones on the thighs of his trousers and held them to the light. No, nothing, he told them. But when they sat in their camps and looked up from the valley late at night, a light still burned in the agent's cabin and they could see him holding their stones to his oil flame and talking to their earth in his skinned and weary voice.

At first the sorted, worthless plugs were dumped each day in a rough pile at the side of the cabin. The clays of the valley consorted with the volcanic earths of Ibela-hoy. Flints jostled sandstones, topsoils ran loose amongst clods, the rounded pebbles of the river bed bubbled in the wasteland shales. He was struck how – held and turned in the daylight – each stone was a landscape. Here was a planet, a globe, with the continents grey and peninsular, the seas cold and smooth to the touch. And here a coastline, one face the beach, four faces cliff, and a rivulet of green where the children and donkeys could make their descent. And here, twisted and smoothed by the survey drill, were the muddied banks of rivers and the barks of trees modelled and reduced in deep, toffee earth. But in the dump, their shapes and colours clashed and were indecent. He remembered how, when he was a child, they had buried his father. The grave was open when the body came.

There were clays and flints piled on the yellow grass. The bottom of his father's trench had filled with water. The digger's spade had severed stones. They said that, in ancient times when humankind went naked and twigged for termites and ate raw meat, the dead were left where they fell. What the animals did not eat became topsoil, loam. The company agent had wished for that, had dreamed of his father free of his grave and spread out on the unbroken ground as calm and breathless as frost. But he could not look at that open grave, those wounded flints, without tears. He could not look at road works, either. Or a ploughed field. Or a broken wall, And whenever he had stared at that squinting corner of his room where the ceiling plaster had fallen and the broken roof laths stuck through, his chest (what was the phrase?) shivered like a parched pea and he dare not sleep. The ceiling doesn't leak, his mother said. It's you that leaks, not it.

Now he wept when he passed the waste pile, when he was drawn at night to stand before it with a lamp or summoned to salvage one lonely stone for his pocket or his table. Sometimes it seemed that the pile was an open wound or an abattoir of stones. But the longer he stood the more it seemed that a piece of the world had been misplaced and abandoned at his cabin side.

Then he took a spade and dug a pit behind the waste pile. First he gathered the chipped yellow stones which lay on the surface and placed them together in a bucket. And then he removed the thin soil crust and piled it neatly on to a tarpaulin. Each individual layer was dug out and piled separately, until the pit was shoulder deep. The continents

146

and planets, the landscapes and coastlines of the waste dump were shovelled into the pit and one by one, in order, the layers of Ibela-hoy were put back in place. Then he scattered the chipped yellow stones on to the bulging ground.

When the gangs delivered drill cores they noticed that the waste had gone. I buried it, he said. I put it back. He showed them where the swollen ground was settling. Well, they said, that's very neat and tidy. Or, Is that what you're paid to do, fool about with spades? His replies made no sense to them. They continued to talk with him roughly or to humour him with banter. What should we do for him, they asked amongst themselves, to bring him back to earth? Should we write, they wondered, to his wife and children or to the boss? Should we let him be and let the illness pass? Some of the kinder, older men went to talk with him, to offer help, to exchange a word or two about the samples on his bench. Yet he seemed indifferent to them and those funnels of earth and stone which could earn them all a fortune. Was that the yellow of bauxite or the rose of cinnabar or the fire-blue of opal? The company agent did not seem to share their excitement or their interest. But when at last they left him in peace he turned to the samples on his bench and sorted through them with unbroken attention. A stone of apple-green he removed and walked with it into the valley where in a cave there were lichens of the same colour. A fistful of grit he scattered in the grass so that it fell amongst the leaf joints like sleet. A round stone he placed on the river bed with other round stones. A grey landscape in an inch of granite

147

he stood in the shadow of the greyest rock. A chip of pitchblende was reunited with black soil.

Once a month when his provisions were delivered together with letters from home, the company agent presented his report and sent back to the city any minerals or gemstones which were worthy of note. Once he had found a fragment of platinum in a sample from the plateau beyond the hill. He and the gang waited a month for the company's response. Low quality platinum, they said. No use to us. And once he had identified graphite amongst the native carbons. But, again, the company was unimpressed. Now he wrapped a piece of damp clay and placed it in a sample bag. Its colours were the colours of pomegranate skins. Its odour was potatoes. He sealed the bag and sent it to the company. Urgent, he wrote on the label. Smell this! And, in the second month, he sent them a cube of sandstone and wrote: See the landscape, the beach, the pathway through the rocks. And later they received the palmful of pebbles that they had requested in his dream.

Alarms rang. Secretaries delivered the agent's file to the company bosses. They searched the certificates and testimonials for any criminal past. Was he a radical? Had he been ill? What should they make of clay, sandstone, pebbles? They called his mother to the offices and questioned her. She showed them her son's monthly letters and pointed to those parts where he spoke of insomnia, an abattoir of stones and a family that never was. He misses home, she said. Why would he send worthless soil and cryptic notes in sample bags? She could not say, except that he had always been a good man, quick to tears. If he had only married, found a girl to love, had children perhaps . . . then who can guess what might have been? But worthless soil? Still she could not say.

The bosses sent their man to Ibela-hoy in their air-conditioned jeep to bring the agent home and to discover what went on. The brick and tarmac of the town and villages lasted for a day. The bosses' man passed the night at the Rest House where the valley greens rose to the implacable evening monochromes of the hills. In the morning, early, he drove on to the bouldered track along the valley side. The Hill Without a Hat swung across his windscreen in the distance. On the summit of the ridge the track widened and cairns marked the route down into the valley of Lekadeeb and then up again towards Ibela-hoy. He stood with his binoculars and sought out the company agent's cabin in the hollow of the hill. He saw the company mobile parked at the door and the antics of men who seemed intoxicated with drink or horseplay. A survey team had returned from the far valley bluffs some days ahead of schedule and hurried to the agent's cabin. The men were wild. They had found silver. They had recognised small fragments in their drill cores and had excavated in the area for larger quantities. They placed a half-dozen jagged specimens on the company agent's bench. Tell us it isn't silver, they challenged him. He looked at one piece of silver shaped like a stem of ginger but metallic grey in colour with puddles of milky-white quartz. What he saw was a bare summit of rock in sunshine. But snow in its crevices was too cold to melt. I'll do some tests, he said.

The men sat outside in their drilling mobile and waited for his confirmation that at last their work had produced minerals of great value. There were bonuses to be claimed, fortunes to be made, celebrations, hugging, turbulent reunions with wives and children to anticipate. The company agent turned the snowy summit in his hand and divined its future. And its past. Once the word Silver was spoken in the company offices, Ibela-hoy could count on chaos; there would be mining engineers, labour camps, a village, roads, bars, drink, soldiers. Bulldozers would push back the soil and roots of silver would be grubbed like truffles from the earth. Dynamite, spoil heaps, scars. And he, the company agent, the man who spilled the beans, would have no time to reconcile the stones, the dreams, the family, the fatigue, the sleeplessness which now had reached its final stage. The turmoil had begun already. He heard the smooth engine of the company jeep as it laboured over the final rise before the cabin. He saw the bosses' man climb out with his folder and his suit and pause to talk with the men who waited inside the mobile's cab. Arms were waved and fingers pointed towards the bluffs where silver lay in wait.

I'll put it back, he said.

By the time the bosses' man had walked into the cabin with a string of false and reassuring greetings on his lips, the company agent had pocketed the half-dozen pieces of silver and had slipped away into the rocks behind the cabin. He climbed as high as was possible without breaking cover and crouched in a gulley. He toyed with the stones on the ground, turning them in his palms, and waited for night. He watched as the bosses' man ran from the cabin and the survey gang jumped from their mobile and searched the landscape for the agent. He watched as they showed the bosses' man where he had buried the waste heap, the world misplaced. He watched as the gang brought picks and shovels, and (insensitive to topsoils and chipped yellow stones) dug into the abattoir. He watched the bosses' man crouch and shake his head as he sorted through the debris for the gold, the agate, the topaz which the men promised had been buried, hidden, there. It was, they said, a matter for the madhouse or the militia. They'd watched the agent for a month or two. He had hugged boulders. He had hidden gemstones, their gemstones, company gemstones, throughout the valley. They'd seen him walking, crouching, placing gemstones in the shade of rocks, in the mouth of caves, under leaves.

A bare summit of rock in sunshine was the location of his dream. There were crevices of unbroken snow and pats of spongy moss. He was naked. There were no clothes. He squatted on his haunches and chipped at flints. Someone had caught a hare – but nobody yet knew how to make fire, so its meat was ripped apart and eaten raw. They washed it down with snow. The carcass was left where it fell. The two boys played with twigs. The baby stood on crescent legs and tugged at grass. He and the woman delved in the softer earth for roots to eat and found silver, a plaything for the boys. He conjured in his dream a world where the rocks were hot and moving, where quakes and

151

volcanoes turned shales to schists, granite to gneiss, limestone to marble, sandstone to quartz, where continents sank and rose like kelp on the tide.

When it was light, he unwrapped himself from the embrace of the boulder where he had passed the night and began to traverse the valley towards the high ground and the rocks where snow survived the sun. His aimless walks had made his legs strong and his mind was soaring with a fever of sleeplessness. He walked and talked, his tongue guiding his feet over the rocks, naming what passed beneath. Molten silicates, he said, as his feet cast bouncing shadows over salt and pepper rocks. Pumice, he said to the hollows. Grass.

In two hours the company agent had reached the ridge where the winds seemed to dip and dive and hug the earth. He turned to the south and, looking down into the valley, he saw the men and the trucks at his cabin and the twist of smoke as breakfast was prepared. Bring my wife and children, he said. And one man, standing at the hut with a hot drink resting on the bonnet of the air-conditioned jeep, saw him calling there and waved his arms. Come down, he said. Come back.

But the company agent walked on until he found that the earth had become slippery with ice and the air white like paper. He looked now for grey rocks, metallic grey, and found them at the summit of his walk, his rendezvous. There was no easy path; the boulders there were shoulder height and he was forced to squeeze and climb. But his hands were taking hold of crevices fossilised with snow and soon, at last, he stood upon the landscape that he had sought, glistening, winking grey with puddles of milky-white quartz. He took the six jagged specimens from his pocket. I am standing here, he said, pointing at an ounce of silver. He took the pieces and placed them in a streak of snow where their colours matched the rock and where, two paces distant, they disappeared for good.

In the afternoon he watched the first helicopter as it beat about the hills, its body bulbous-ended like a floating bone. And then, close by, he heard the grinding motors of the jeep as it found a route between the rocks and stalled. He heard voices and then someone calling him by his first name. Was it his son? He walked to the edge of his grey platform and looked down on the heads of the bosses' man, a soldier and two of the survey gang. Climb down, they said. We're going to take you home. A holiday. I have my job to do, he said. Yes, they said, we all have jobs to do. We understand. But it's cold up here and you must be tired and hungry. Climb down and we'll drive you back to the city. No problems. No awkward questions. Your mother's waiting. Just show us what is hidden and you can be with your family.

Bring my family here, he said. Bring my wife and children here. The men looked at each other and then one of the survey gang spoke. You have no wife and children, he said. You lied. The company agent picked up the largest stone and flung it at the men. It landed on the bonnet of the jeep and its echo was as metallic, as full of silver, as the grey hill.

Leave him there, they said. Let hunger bring him down. It was cold that night above Ibela-hoy. But there was

153

warmth in numbers. The company agent and his wife encircled their children, their breath directed inwards, their backs turned against the moon. And in the morning when the sun came up and the colours of the hill and its valley accelerated from grey and brown, to red and green, to white, the company agent gathered stones for his family and they breakfasted on snow.